RAMBLIN' ON

TALES OF A FARM BOY GROWING UP

These stories were written covering a span of time
from 1930 to 2001 pertaining, for the most part, to fun
times such as hunting, fishing and traveling.

BY
Dale Walker

Library of Congress Control Number: 2002090896
ISBN: 0-9718027-0-X

Printed in the United States by:
Morris Publishing
3212 East Highway 30
Kearney, NE 68847
1-800-650-7888

FOREWORD

Over the years during family gatherings and sometimes sitting around the supper table after a meal of fried venison, mashed potatoes and brindle gravy, Daddy would entertain us with stories about his boyhood growing up with three older brothers on a farm in Texas. There was a never ending supply of the anecdotes on hunting, fishing, traveling, farming and boyhood antics and they all gave voice to his memories. He had a knack for transforming ordinary experiences into fascinating word pictures so that we didn't miss having TV or radio. He could go on for hours until bath time and bedtime called us away.

As we got older, we began to feel a need to keep these stories as a part of our family history - as colorful as any scrapbook full of snapshots.

His artistic talent has blossomed late in life as can be noted throughout the book containing his original and quite humorous illustrations.

As he began to record his stories, the sixty plus year old manual U.S. Royal typewriter on the kitchen table gave way to a computer key board and this collection of stories is the result.

Even Daddy's Email messages are entertaining and can bring a smile in the midst of a hectic workday. If any one of us lets more than a few days go by without answering his Email, he is likely to send a reminder saying "I guess high water must have gotten over your mail machine. Whenever you dry it out and get it back in working order, give me a holler."

He continues to spin his tales that relate his on-going experiences. We hope that you will get as much enjoyment out of reading them as we have in hearing them.

Thanks Daddy. We love you - and we're ready for Volume 2.

Nancy, Rosemary and Ed

DEDICATION

When I think of the people who inspired me to write this book, I think of my daughter Rosemary. She kept after me for several years to write down my life's stories and I kept thinking that would be very awkward to do. I'd be plowing or some other field work and when I thought of some tale, stop and write a little. I just didn't have time for such as that.

One day my wife's sister Lee Ruby, handed me a pocket size tape recorder and said, "here, I'm not using this and you keep it in your pocket and do like Rosemary wants you to do." OK, when I started talking to the recorder, I couldn't find a place to stop. One story reminded me of another. Mind you, I didn't do it while plowing.

My grandson Matthew who is blind and has a computer that talks to him said he would type the stories for me. I filled thirteen one hour tapes and Matthew typed every word that I put on them. When he got them all typed and printed, he sent them to me. When I started reading them I knew right away that I couldn't put "this stuff" in a book. You just don't write like you talk. It just comes out different. So, I went through them and retyped them. I had an awful time typing - I could type pretty well but was used to a manual machine and leaned on the keys heavily and that didn't work on an electric typewriter. I ended up with a lot of erased and painted out characters - many of them.

I called two different publishing companies and they sent me a lot of information. One of the things they stressed was, by all means if you choose to "self publish" a book, use a computer to type it. But if you have to use a type writer, make sure it is an electric one. Well, I had a friend (Terry Fatherree) who had a computer and I thought I would get her to type it for me. When I asked her, she told me that she couldn't do it because her computer was down. OK, I decided to buy a computer and make myself learn not to lean on the keys. I learned a little but the thing I liked about it is that the corrections are so easy to make. My friend Eric Turner took me to San Antonio and he picked out what he thought I needed and we came home with it. Now, Eric got himself into this and he was very good to come over and help me learn. Thanks Eric. Without you, I probably wouldn't be doing anything but leaning on my keys.

My wife and I went over my writings and corrected the misspelled words (all we could see) and corrected some grammar. I printed up two copies and sent one each to Rosemary and Evelyn Kingsbery. Rosemary came up with a lot of suggestions and suggested some different phrasing in some stories. Evelyn marked the misspelled words she saw but suggested very little else. She said that she didn't want to change my style of writing. I didn't know I had a style. Thanks Evelyn.

Speaking of grammar, it's not that I didn't have good English teachers in school because I had two of the very best. It was just that I wasn't a good student. One of those teachers still lives here in town - Miss. McGillivray - later Mrs. Lunz. Thanks to you Mrs. Lunz for what you did teach me. I remember a little of it.

Thanks go to all my family because you are all a very important part of my life.

CONTENTS

AN ARMADILLO TALE

We lived in town until I was six years old. In the spring of 1930, after my brothers, John, Jim and Harold got out of school, we moved to the farm. I was to start school in the fall. Before moving to the farm though, Dad would go out there to work and sometimes we all went. My Granddad and Grandmother lived out there and we would eat the noon meal with them. I was too young to do much work so I got to play a lot. My brothers had an air rifle and sometimes I would get to shoot it. This one time I took it out hunting by myself. There was a field we called "river field" that still had some brush in it, and that was where I was hunting. I came upon an armadillo that was rooting in the dirt, feeding on roots and bugs. I stood still and he worked up real close to me. Then I shot him right between the eyes. Boy, he was jumping, flopping, and throwing blood everywhere. After he quit moving, I took him to Granddad's house to show him off.

Dad had made baskets out of armadillo shells and they were really nice. He shaped them over an object and then, pointing the head up and bringing the tail over to the head, this would form the handle. He lined them with velvet making them very pretty. I suppose bagging that armadillo was just about as exciting to me then as bagging a nice buck now.

CHICKENS WENT BYE-BYE

We hadn't lived at the farm very long - the house was down below the hill. At first the house was just one room - a pretty good-sized room though. It was 14 x 24 and the whole living setup was in there. The kitchen was in the north west corner, the dining room was next to it - north east corner, the bedroom was on the south by two windows with a double bunked bed in the middle of the west wall. The living room was on the east wall or just anywhere you wanted to sit. Outside the house on the east was an arbor with vines growing on it creating shade and a lot of our living was done under it.

Dad was doing some work of some sort there under the arbor and I was playing. I had some pet chickens and they were there too. I had some buckeye seeds in my pocket and I decided to see if the chickens liked them. I mashed them up with a hammer and the chickens ate them. Pretty quick, the chickens started acting funny and soon they were dead. When Dad found out what I had done, he said, "No wonder." Well for sure, I learned a lesson. I never fed buckeyes to anything since then.

RABBITS FOR SUPPER

When I grew big enough to keep up with my older brother, Jim, I'd get to go hunting with him. Sometimes, Dad would let us quit work a little bit early so we could go rabbit hunting. We liked to go up to Del Monte corner which is where highway 1025 comes into 83 and then on west and a little north about another half or three quarters of a mile. Back in the early days there had been a town site laid out there so the brush wasn't too awful thick. This area was good jackrabbit country and we liked to try for them.

Back in 1910 when my mother came to this country there was a hotel and a post office there. There was a flowing water well there and lots of people came there for their drinking water.

We would most always get a couple jacks and maybe a cottontail or two. By now, it was getting dark and we had a mile and a half to get back to the house.

This time period was in the early 30's and the great depression was in full swing and we lived off the land. Mother would make hamburger out of those jackrabbits and make them into meat loaf. The cottontails were fried - number one stuff.

All of this reminds me of the saying; "you make a living by the sweat of the brow." How true that was back in those days.

MY EARLY FARM DAYS

I turned six years old April 5, 1930. We moved to the farm that spring soon after school was out. My three brothers were in school and I started that fall.

My Dad got a job driving the school bus - he had to build his own bus so he bought a Chevrolet truck. It was a cab and chassis and he built the bus body. It was about ten feet long and he built rail seats in it - one on each side and a rail down the middle with a board seat on each side of it. He fixed roll up and down curtains over the windows. It was quite airy in the winter. He drove his bus for three years I think and then the school bought its first busses. There was one other home made bus in operation during that three year period. Bill Bailey was the proud owner of that one. The school purchased four busses - two Fords and two Chevrolets. Dad got one of the Chevrolets. His route was, I believe, everything west of the river and north of town.

The dirt road coming in to our farm was quite new and in wet weather, it was a bad muddy road. It seems that it rained a lot that first year or two because I remember Dad leaving the bus out at the highway and coming to the house in our little '26 Chevrolet. It was a lot easier to get through the mud than was the truck.

During those years of the private owned bus; at the end of the school year, Dad would gather up all the kids and we would go up to the old Batesville river crossing out northeast of La Pryor and have a nice picnic. The parents were invited too and of course most all brought food. We also would have ice cream. That was really fun. I say fun, the water was clear and cool and the sun was hot. Boy, now, you talk about sunburned kids. Along about come home time, everyone began to feel their burning backs and legs. The blisters began to rise - boy, it was a sight. I don't know why there wasn't some supervision used by the adults.

The house we lived in at the farm was a one-room house. A nice size 14 x 24 room but there had to be a kitchen, dining room, living room and a bedroom. The bathroom was a small, very small room at the end of the trail out back. The wall studs and ceiling joists were 4 feet apart and the rafters the same. The walls were of about 10-inch shiplap and the roof was corrugated tin and there were no inner walls or ceiling. The main thing I remember about the house was when we had a thunderstorm with strong winds; the house would weave back and forth. There was one window in the north end, a door and two windows in the south end and a door in the west wall pretty close to the north corner. The arrangement was something like the following: The kitchen was in the northwest corner. The cook stove was a wood burning thing and the cabinets consisted of apple boxes tacked to the wall (then they were wood) with curtains for doors. The dining room right next to the kitchen in the northeast corner. Along the east wall was Mother's piano and living room. On the south by the windows was Mom's and Dad's bed. Our beds were a double bunked structure at about the middle of the west wall. In the dining room there was an oak table that would pull out and I think there were six twelve inch leafs that could be put in it. It would make a fairly long table. There were six chairs. When company came, we kids had to find something else to sit on. Those apple boxes served pretty well.

After a few months, Dad built a kitchen dining room full length on the west side and a sleeping porch full length on the east side. These rooms were 12 feet wide I believe.

In 1932 we had a flood on the river and the water came up under the house and then again in 1933 we had another flood. When one of those floods came, it floated our chicken house enough to turn it over and we lost a lot of chickens. Then, in 1935, we had the big one. It got up in the house about 20 or so inches. It ruined mother's piano. Our beds were up on stilts so mother could store her canned goods under them so the beds didn't get wet. In 1936, the house was moved up on the hill and needless to say why. That move will be described in another story.

BAD TIME GETTING HOME FROM CAMP

Back in 1933 our pastor at the church had a nice group of boys in his Royal Ambassador Chapter. One summer he decided to take the boys to camp. He made arrangements with the Boy Scout camp people, which is on the Nueces River up the other side of Barksdale. Camp Faucet was the name of the camp. Bro. Holloway asked Dad to haul the boys in his bus. Most of them rode in the bus and some rode with the preacher in his Franklin car. I wasn't old enough to be in the chapter but both my Mom and Dad went so I got to go too. Elsie Morris and her sister went to do the cooking and help herd the kids. Alvin Morris will know whom I'm talking about if he ever reads this.

We no sooner got settled into the camp when it started raining. It rained and rained and the river came up. The kids couldn't go swimming or play baseball or anything. We were cut off from town and they couldn't go buy food either. Dad and Bro. Holloway went to some of the ranches to buy some goats or chickens - just anything for food. It seemed they could buy milk but then, who wants to live on milk. Dad did take our big two and a half-gallon ice cream freezer but there was no ice around there. Finally some man told us that he could bring us some ice. Well, he did. I think he had gotten a 50-pound block and put it in a burlap sack and dragged it across the river behind his horse. When he got to us, it was only about 10 pounds. We ended up drinking milk after all.

After three or four days, the water receded enough that Dad and some other men around there thought maybe he could drive the bus across the river. Someone told Dad to get some wax and melt it and coat all the spark plugs and wires - just coat everything while you're at it. He did that and so did Bro. Holloway. The preacher drove in first and right off; his gas tank filled up with water. That put a stop to his car. Luckily there was a guy with a team of mules and he latched on to the Franklin car and pulled it on across. Dad pulled in with the bus and made it all right. Thinking that we would have to pull or push the preacher's car but when we got across the river, the preacher's car was not there. All the kids had gotten out and pushed it up the first hill and then they'd jump in and coast a while and then jump out and push some more and then ride some more. They did that for several miles and had fun doing it. We came to the crossing near Camp Wood and had to do it again. There was a highway department man there and he thought we could make it all right. He had all the kids get to the up side of the bus for weight purposes and we made it across all right. However, in starting across here, Bunch Lunetta was standing on the step where the guide was standing and the guide told him to get out of the way. Instead of getting in the bus, Bunch jumped off into the water. The water was about 18 inches deep going across this slab and there were several tinhorns under the slab. Well, Bunch jumped on the up side and went right into one of these horns. He was gone like a flash but a few seconds later, he came up down below. Luckily, he made it out of there. Everyone who saw this thing happen thought "Oh no," but like I said, he made it out all right and unhurt. There was another crossing and I guess they call it the "nineteen miles." One of these crossings they were pulling us with a team of horses hooked to a wagon and the bus to the wagon. The reach under the wagon broke but Dad was able to make it out under his own power.

By the time we got to the high bridge between Uvalde and La Pryor it had gotten dark. This high bridge was a mile or so up stream from the current bridge on Hwy 83. This bridge was damaged by the high water. The highway department was there too. Part of the floor had been knocked out. It was a narrow gap that was out. The highway people had some big wide planks placed across this gap and we drove across on them.

I mentioned earlier, Elsie Morris and her sister were along helping and doing the cooking. On the way back - doing all these water crossings and things, they had their bathing suits on and riding on the front fenders of the bus and they really got sun burned. The sad part about sunburn is, you don't know you're burned until it is too late.

After getting down in the flat country, the preacher's Franklin had to be pushed the rest of the way home. I guess the high water had just about crested at home when we got there.

MY FIRST BUCK

I was 8 years old going on 9 when I bagged my first buck. My Dad and I went to a friend's place to hunt. We went in the pasture north of his fields and went about a mile north to an area my Dad referred to as the "Sand Hills." This was a very good area to rattle for deer when the rut was on. When we arrived there we climbed up in a big mesquite tree and after getting ourselves positioned Dad began to rattle his deer antlers. Wasn't long at all before he whispered to me, "There's one right under the tree." I turned a little and he said to turn a little more. Well, when I saw the deer and pointed my gun, he broke to run just as I fired. Dad said he'd get down and see if I had hit him or not. Well, when he got down there, he said that I got blood and to come on down. I had gotten the buck all right. I must have shot through some brush before hitting him because I could put my fist in the hole where the bullet went in and nearly took the whole shoulder off the other side. I was using Dad's old hexagon barreled Winchester long gun in .30/.30 caliber. We dressed the deer out and hung him by his antlers in a crotch of the tree.

While we were waiting for the deer to drain out and cool a bit, we walked about 200 yards away and got up in another tree and Dad rattled. We stayed about a half-hour in this tree and then got down to go get our deer and head back to the car. Well, we had walked about half way back to my deer when we heard a noise back behind us. When we looked, a real nice buck turned and ran right from under the tree we had just gotten out of. I don't know what we would have done with two deer. I wasn't big enough to carry a deer by myself. We went and got the one we had hung and Dad carried it and I carried the guns. Those two guns was a pretty good load for me.

MAKING LIGHTNING

When we were kids, we would get a wooden shingle and make arrows out of it. A shingle is thick on one end and thin on the other. We cut about a three inch piece off it and whittle the thick end to a point leaving a notch that would catch on a string loop and make the shaft round leaving a fletching or feather we called it on the thin end. We cut a straight stick about three quarters of an inch in diameter and tied a rubber band about a half inch wide and about fifteen inches long tying a loop of strong string on the other end. Stick/handle on one end of rubber band and the loop on the other end to catch the notch on the arrow's point. This type thing was suitable for hunting rabbits or any sort of small game. The rubber bands were cut from rubber inner tubes. We also used this type rubber band on the plain old slingshots. (Didn't call them slingshots back in those days. Some of you old timers will remember what we called them - I can't remember). I mentioned hunting rabbits - that was ok because you could find most of your arrows. Shooting at birds wasn't done much because you lost too many arrows.

Now we'll get into the recipe for making lightning. We would get an old Ford model "T" ignition coil and in that coil were coils of copper wire. One of the coils was made up of very fine wire - we called it "hair wire." We'd take about fifty feet of this fine wire and tie it to one of these arrows and shoot it up over the highline and we created lightning. This seemed like great fun but when Dad caught us doing it, it all stopped.

Later on, my three brothers, John, Jim, and Harold found a way to create much greater lightning. There was a shed about half way between our house and Granddad's house. We had corn stored in this shed and one day we four boys were down there shucking corn. My brothers got to throwing baling wire up over the highline that went along the road and was close to the shed. That size wire, when it fell over two highline wires made a pretty good light and popping noise too. One of them picked up an old windshield frame and John threw it up and it caught over two highline wires; it popped alright, but this time it burned the highline cable in two. The line lay on the ground hissing, popping, and moving around like a snake. Jim went down to Granddad's house to the telephone and called CP&L (Power Company) and told them that something had happened to the highline. It was getting late and we went up to do our chores and eat supper. After supper, John, Jim and Harold decided to go down and watch CP&L work on the line. They hid in the brush while watching and listening to the repairmen. They heard one of them say, "Wonder how this thing burned in two?" I had stayed at the house because Mother wouldn't let me go and besides that, she figured something was going on and she made me tell her what had happened. Boy, when the three came back to the house, Mother told them, "You just wait till Dad comes home." Dad had gone fishing with Uncle Ruben Donnell and wouldn't be back till late that night. Now, you talk about some kids begging! They begged pretty hard and promised not to ever do anything like that again. After a good bit of begging, Mother finally said, "If you think you've learned a lesson, I won't tell." They assured her that they would never, never do anything like that again.

A lot of years later, we were all together: I guess it was twenty or more years and we all were married and all four of us were back from WWII. We were sitting around the dinner table out at the farm and this story came up. Dad was sitting there listening and I noticed his eyebrows sorta wrinkled up and I could just hear him saying, "dad-gone kids."

A DEMOLISHED BICYCLE

During grammar school years I had friends who would come out to spend the night with me and sometimes I would get to go to their house. However, that was very seldom because I had my chores to do and if I was gone, that meant someone had to double for me. That usually meant my mother and she had plenty of other work to do. There were two boys who were twins; their names were Bert and Simon Smith. One or the other of them would come out from time to time. Either one of them was always ready to help me with my work. If there was any time left, we would grab a gun and go rabbit hunting or get a pole and go fishing. Sometimes, we'd go horseback riding.

Simon was out there this one time. Early the next morning we had a little time after eating breakfast and doing the chores before we had to make a run for the school bus. Simon wanted to ride the horse and I was going to ride the bicycle. Well, he got on the pony and she liked to run full blast, so he just lets her go. We were going down to Granddad's house about a half mile and I had gotten about a third of the way down there when he was coming back to meet me. I was in the right track and he was coming in my track, so I moved over to the left and so did he. I moved back to the right and he moved too. As we both moved again, time had run out and we hit head on. The bicycle went about ten yards over to my right and Simon went flying through the air and the horse and I piled up together. None of us was hurt. Oh, we had a few bruises and scratches. Anyhow, our playtime was up so we had to run like heck to get to the school bus. We had to go a half-mile to catch it.

How we survived some of those stunts and grow up, I'll never know.

BIRDSHOT PATTERN IN THE OUTHOUSE

I was in the seventh grade in the old red grammar school building here in Crystal City when this story occurred. A friend came out to spend the night with me. He lived out east of town on the Noah White farm; I can't remember his name. As I remember, he had recently come here from Nebraska. Some of you may know the place as the Melvin Peters place.

I told him a bunch of stuff about some guy and my Dad feuding. To make it look real, I had fired a load of bird shot through the open door and into the back of the outhouse. I told him that one morning before daylight this guy thought my Dad was sitting in there and he shot in there.

The thing that really makes this story seem real is - we had a very green yard and a lot of rabbits came to graze. Most every morning Dad would take his .22 rifle just about daylight, and shoot a rabbit or two. Sure enough, the next morning a little shooting took place. Boy, you talk about a kid squeezing in under a bed in no time flat! He wouldn't come out real soon either.

FIRST RIVER TRIP FOR TWO BOYS

When I was about seven years old my Dad, Mother and brother Jim planned a trip down the river. Dad borrowed a boat from the Miller brothers who lived across the street from Bill Brennan's machine shop. The boat was twelve feet long and pointed in front with straight up and down sides and square back end. Really not the best engineered shaped boat one could build.

Dad would get carbide cans at the machine shop for the purpose of storing our food. These cans were about two feet high and about fourteen inches in diameter and had screw in lids with a gasket which made them air tight. We used these just in case the boat turned over. We would go up near La Pryor and put the boat in the river. This was at the north side of the 7D ranch, which was also called the "Game Preserve". The Nueces River is a state river so we had the right to fish it and to camp within its banks.

The water was running fairly strong and that meant you could float over the rapids pretty easy but also meant, there were more potential hazards. We came to a tree that had fallen and pretty well blocked the river. Dad was in the front and Jim in back. Dad was picking his way through the tree and Jim was holding to a limb and Dad told Jim to let it go - let it go. Well, when he let it go it lowered the back end and the water came in and took it under very quickly. There was a limb there just in the right place for Mother and me to grab onto. The bedroll came up behind mother's legs and nearly dragged her down but she managed to hang on. I had gotten a brand new straw hat and I lost it. I remember crying about that. Well, somehow, they got the boat on through the tree and then the loss was assessed. Most of the cooking gear was lost including the coffeepot. The skillet had lodged under one of the seats. The knives and forks were in one of the cans so were retrieved later. You remember about the cans that I spoke of - now you know why. The bedroll was wet through but it dried pretty easy. Did you ever hear of skillet coffee? You have now. We finally reached the Evans Lake and that's where we made camp, caught minnows and fished.

13

The Evans Lake is a beautiful piece of water with beautiful willow trees dipping into its edges with lily pads in spots in the shallow places. Pecan trees towering high into the sky on the first and second banks. The lake is something like two thirds of a mile in length. At the lower end, the water goes down a long rapid and is an excellent place to catch minnows and to play.

We were fishing with cane poles using minnows for bait. We were setting in the boat parked along a big log angling into the water. Jim pulled his line up to check the bait and I put my line over where his was and right away, I caught a nice catfish. Needless to say, he complained about me getting his place. Somehow, I got my line back in his place in a little bit and caught another nice fish. Boy, he really complained then. It was a good thing Dad was in the boat too or I might have been exterminated.

I don't remember much about the rest of the trip. One thing though, when we got far enough down river to where the banks were much higher and the river had less fall we began finding log jams. Also, it was much hotter because being down in a deeper cut, the wind was blocked off.

About nine years later, a friend of mine came to visit. Billy McFall was his name. The McFall family had lived here several years earlier. His dad was Kelly McFall and worked for CP&L. He delivered ice around town with a team of mules and "the ice wagon." They moved to Beeville, Texas and later to Corpus Christi.

Billy came up for the summer and as we were working on the farm, we talked about coming down the river. We asked Dad about it and he told us if we got our work done we could do it. He laid out a batch of work for us to do, which took about a week to do. Well, we worked like everything to get it done so we could go. I don't know if that would be called strategy or not, but the work got done.

A good friend of ours, Charlie Strolger had a boat that he had built. It was ten feet long and twenty-eight inches wide at the bottom. We borrowed that and packed up a couple cans with food and things that we didn't want to get wet in case of a "shipwreck". We traveled light in those days - no motor or gas, no water- we drank river water, no ice chest, and only a small canvas to sleep on and cover with. Boy, did we ever get chiggers in those days! We'd scratch for a month after those trips.

The only fishing gear we carried was a couple cane poles and twenty setlines. We had spent about half the night before catching frogs. We arrived at Evans Lake about mid afternoon and set up camp. Wasn't much to set up - put the canvas on the ground and fix a place for a fire to cook on. We set our twenty lines out and got them baited just about dark and went to camp and tried to sleep. We didn't check the lines in the night. If we had, we might have gotten more fish. Next morning, we were going around checking our lines and taking them up. Billy was pulling them in and wrapping them on a board. I think we had gotten to the last one or nearly the last one - it showed no movement until he got it part way in (thank goodness, he wasn't untying them first) and then it started pulling slowly but surely and he couldn't hold it. It was slipping through his fingers as he was trying to hold it and burned his fingers pretty good. He let go of it then and when all the slack was taken up, the willow limb it was tied to went right on down into the water. Billy stuttered some and by now, he really was stuttering and telling me to get it. I let the boat come around to where I was next to the limb. When it came back up enough to where I could take hold of the line I could feel something on it but it wasn't fighting. I could tell it was heavy. When I got it up enough to see it a little, I didn't know what it was for a second. I knew I didn't want to put my hands on it. I guess the fish had been on for several hours and was played out. I told Billy to give me another line - I dropped it down and got it hooked in his mouth and with the two lines, I pulled him on board. Biggest dagone thing I'd ever seen! It was a flat head cat and measured 44 inches long and 28 inches around the middle. He was much longer than the boat was wide. We put a dog leash chain on him and tied him to the back of the boat. We were about 200 yards from camp and it took us a long time to paddle back with the fish pulling this way and that every once in a while.

We needed to get started on down river - we had to get to the

Butler hole for the second night. We didn't know just how to go about handling the fish - we knew we had to keep him alive because we had no ice to pack it in. We put him in a toe sack and dragged him that way. At least he couldn't pull us around. Every time we came to a rapid, we'd pick him up and put him on the boat seat so he wouldn't get bruised. We reached the Butler hole all right by putting in a hard day's work. We took the fish out of the sack and staked him out on a good strong rope. The next morning, he was fairly fresh and gave us a pretty good fight when we brought him in.

The Butler hole was considered, to me, to be the changing spot of the river from rocky bottom and rapids to mud bottom and log jams. That day we needed to get to the lower end of the Ray place. Just a little ways before reaching that point, there was a fellow by the name of Ace Green camped permanently on the west side of the river. He heard us coming and came down to the river to see who we were. We showed him our fish and he said he thought it would weigh around 50 pounds. Billy and I had gotten his weight up to 75 pounds - we had lifted him into the boat and out so many times - he just got bigger all the time. After visiting with Ace a little while, we went on to the Ray place and staked the fish out once again, parked the boat and headed out for home to get the truck. It must have been at least 10 miles to home and I don't remember if we walked all the way, caught a ride or if Dad met us. At any rate, we had to get to the house because we had to get ice to pack the fish in. We got all the ice out of the trays at home, and out of Granddad's box and our neighbors down below us and headed back to get our stuff. First thing we did was to dress the fish. We laid him on the boat seat and field dressed him just about like you'd dress a deer. When we got home, we weighed him and he went 45 pounds field dressed. Dad said we could call him 50 pounds - the guts would go at least 5 pounds.

In a couple days, we had a fish fry. Mother invited a bunch of people from the church and of course my Granddad and the neighbors from whom we had gotten some ice. There were 35 guest who came. We fried the fish in an old wash pot and you talk about something good - it was. After everyone got their fill of fish, there was a large mixing bowl full left over.

Billy and I thought we did pretty good for a couple of rookie boys.

RATTLESNAKE IN THE TRAIL

I spoke of Jess Nash in another story. This time, Jim and I went up there to take a little hunt. To the north about a half to one mile, there was what we called, "the sand hills" and this was really good buck country in the winter. My Dad took me up there when I was eight years old and I bagged my first buck there. This time however, we went east to a tank to watch for deer. The weather was warm and the chances of seeing deer were pretty good. We waited until good dark and hadn't seen anything so we decided to go back. We were walking along a gas pipeline to the west until we came to a small line taking off the big one going to Jess's house. There was a little-used car trail we were walking in. In a little while, a rattlesnake went off up ahead of us. We were used to this sort of thing and I'm telling you, it doesn't take you long to put it in reverse. Jim was in the right track and I was in the left. Somehow in the process of ginning backwards, we got tangled up with one another. Jim lay there unconscious and I was sitting there laughing and the snake was still rattling up ahead. Course we had gone backwards five or so yards. In a little while Jim came around and asked if I had killed the snake. I said no, but I would. Jim had a big goose egg on his forehead and I think when he fell, he brought his gun up and hit himself across his forehead. He thought that I hit him with the butt of my gun. I think if I had hit him like that, it would have cut his head. The ole boots that I had on, had steel cleats on the heels and I had stepped on one of his hands and really cut it bad.

We gathered ourselves together, killed the snake and went on. When we got home, we told Mother and Dad that we had gotten into a fight with a game warden. Really got them shook up. I don't know why they didn't shoot us for all the stuff we told them all the time.

THREE HIGH SCHOOL BOYS GO CAMPING

When I was a junior in high school two other boys and I planned a camping trip as soon as school was out. The other two were Robert McNeil and Jim Riggs.

When school was out that spring, we were packed and were off to the hills. We went to Uvalde, then up to the 19-mile crossing on the Nueces River and then a little farther north to the Stoner Ranch. The river ran through this ranch and the huge pecan trees afforded a beautiful place to camp and fish. When we arrived, we went to the headquarters to get permission to be there. We talked to Mr. Stoner and he told us it would be ok. As I remember, he was working some goats so we offered our help. I remember wrestling some of those things to the ground and getting skinned up a little but I guess we had fun. Mr. Stoner was probably glad when we left to go camp. We went down and made camp under some of those beautiful trees.

We were going to be real smart and not get sunburned so we left our shirts on. We didn't think about our legs and I want to tell you, that night we had blisters on our legs as big as saucers. How could we be so smart? Boy, we suffered for that mistake. The second day there, a big thunder storm was coming up and we got scared the river might come on a rise so we decided to go across the river on higher ground to camp. We had forded the river and it wouldn't have taken much of a rise to cut us off. On this side there was not a good place to camp. There were no shade trees so we just had to grin and bear it. However fishing was better on this side as the water was deeper. Next day we had gotten a real nice bunch of perch and fried them for lunch. We had a pie plate full and heaping with fried fish. The flies were bad so we had a cup towel over the fish. One of us, I don't remember which, pulled the towel up to get some fish and somehow it turned the pan over and there went our fish into the dirt. That one made us real happy. We managed to salvage some of the fish but it wasn't enough. I guess we filled up on bread.

We stayed three nights and then headed home. We had gone in my Dad's little 1926 Chevy that used to be a turtle back thing but had been made into a little flat bed truck thing. The seat was made of boards. No top but did have a windshield. We had taken a boat with us but didn't use it. Coming home as we came through Uvalde, we came Down Park Street in order to stay out of main town. Where Park Street crossed Highway 90 there was a stop sign. Just to the left, there was a service station and a State Trooper was sitting there. The exhaust pipe had fallen off the manifold and as we pulled away from the stop sign, the noise got the attention of the trooper. Well, you guessed it. He came up on us pretty quick and stopped us. He said we were disturbing the peace. We showed him and explained how the exhaust pipe had fallen off the manifold. I think he was about to let us go when he noticed there were farm license plates on our vehicle and we had a boat on board and you are not to mix farm license with having pleasure. Well, he issued me a ticket for incorrect license registration. When we got home, we figured Jim Rigg's dad could get things fixed up, as he was a U.S. Deputy Marshall. When we got home, Mr. Riggs was out of town on business so Mrs. Riggs said she'd go up to Uvalde and fix things up. She went the next day but upon her return she tells us we had to pay the fine. They did change the charge to a lesser offense which was disturbing the peace. She went ahead and paid the fine which was around $80.00. We divided it up among the three of us and vowed we'd be more careful next time.

MAIN EVENTS BETWEEN 1935 AND 1999

After the big flood in 1935, Dad and Mother talked about moving the house up on the hill. Dad had traded for 25 acres of land just north of our property and it had a nice hill on it. Talk was cheap so that is about all that happened – talk. We had some friends who lived in Carrizo Springs whom we visited quite a lot. One day in their presence Dad was talking about what we needed to do about the house but he didn't have the money nor did he have any equipment to do something like that. These people's name was Strippling. Less was a well driller and had all kinds of heavy equipment and he told Dad, "This summer if I'm caught up on my drilling, we are going to move this house up on that hill." Dad told him again that he didn't have any money to do it with. Less said again that we were going to move this house up there. Sure enough, he brought his equipment over and the house was moved.

They moved it in three pieces and in setting it up, the two side rooms were set at the same level as the center room instead of a step down into those rooms.

Later on a screened porch was added onto the front and a bathroom added to the north end of the bedrooms and then a nice storeroom onto the north of the kitchen.

My oldest brother John engineered the yard. We had a dirt scoop we pulled with the tractor. It took one driving the tractor and one handling the scoop. After he leveled it he put a border around it so we could flood it. We planted trees and carpet grass and Mother wanted an arbor on the west side of the house. That was built and she planted grapes all along it. We pumped water from the tank below and flooded the yard every week and it didn't take long until we had grass, grapes, and trees.

The grass got so rank it really became a chore to mow it with the old push mower. Had to mow pretty often or you were in trouble. Finally, Dad got a power mower and lessened that chore considerable.

We built the cow pens out north and a little east of the house on a sloping area so they would drain when it rained. We put a lane over on the east side a little ways to bring the cattle up from

21

the fields.

We milked several cows and we ran the milk through a cream separator. We drank lots of milk. Mother would always have a pitcher of chocolate syrup so we could have "chocolate milk." Now that was good stuff. We didn't drink the separated milk; we drank the good whole stuff. The calves and hogs got the separated milk.

Most of the time we milked ten or twelve cows. These cows were Jersey and gave very rich milk. The cream that was separated was very heavy and thick and was high in butterfat. Mother made lots of butter and sold it to people in town - some of that rich cream she sold too. We also had chickens and sold lots of eggs and those hens when they got old, sure did make good "chicken and dumplings." Mother and Dad made their living mostly by selling butter and eggs until the mid-70's after which they completely retired.

My oldest brother John graduated from high school in 1935. He went into the army and was stationed at Fort Sam Houston in San Antonio. He attended a Prep School which would enter him into OCS (officer's candidate school) if he had graduated with high enough honors. Almost but not quite. After getting out of the army, he went to Texas A&M and earned a degree in Mechanical Engineering. After his graduation from A & M, he worked for an Aircraft Company. The war was on so Uncle Sam was soon ready for him to come visit.

My twin brothers graduated from high school in 1937. Harold went into the Air Corp and was stationed at Kelly Field near San Antonio. When his three-year hitch was up, World War II was close at hand so he stayed in and finally satisfied his heart's desire by becoming a pilot and went through all sorts of experiences. He made many missions flying the Burma Hump but he told of some pretty good experiences right here in the states. Jim had worked for Keith and Roberts for a year or two while he was still in school and after his graduation, Roberts put him in Carrizo Springs managing their store there. After the war broke out, he went into the Navy. After his boot training, he served on a Mine Sweeper in the Atlantic. After he came home from war, Roberts put him in the manager's position of the

Western Auto Store here in Crystal. After I graduated from high school, I went to visit Uncle Sam also. I was in the Air Force in an outfit called "Army Airways Communication Service." Later, they changed its name to "Airways Communication System." I don't know why the change in name, the job stayed the same. My overseas service was in the ETO (European Theater of Operations). I got out of the service in November 1946.

When I returned home, I went to Temple, Texas where Ruth was just about finished with her Medical Technologist training. About one year earlier (I think it was the night before Christmas) I was sent to the states. After you had served a period of time overseas and got to the states for any reason, you automatically got a furlough. As I mentioned, I got home the night before Christmas. Ruth managed to come to the train station in San Antonio with my brothers to pick me up. That night was the only time we had to talk because she had to return to Temple on Christmas day in order to be in training the day after. We agreed that I would come up to Temple toward the weekend and we'd go get our licenses and get married. We tied the knot January 1, 1946.

I was discharged in November 1946 and before I came home Ruth had rented an apartment and that is where we met. The next day, I went to Waco where my brother John was taking postgraduate work. He had bought a 1934 two-door Ford car to fix up and sell. He had written me that he had it and I could have it and pay him what he had in it. I paid him and still had to get more parts to fix it. It took me a couple days to fix it and I got it done just in time for us to drive home for Thanksgiving. The old thing did very well. It still had the back glass out of it but the car had an exhaust heater and we kept quite warm on our trip home. She finished her training in December '46 and we came home to stay. She went to work for Doctor Poindexter the first of January, '47 here in Crystal and I ventured into the business world. I purchased a service station. I became dissatisfied with the service station and in about a year I sold it.

I purchased a hay baler and a small tractor and baled hay. That led to other things. I managed to get a larger tractor and disc and started doing plowing. Through the years after more equipment was collected, I guess you could call me a "Custom Farm Operator." I did this until my retirement in the mid-90's. Ruth retired along about this time too and then we started doing what we had always wanted to do - be together all the time. Oh, I still farm in my back yard and she farms her flower beds in the front yard. However, we can keep check on each other pretty well.

Ruth and I bought the home place from my parents back in 1970. We added to the farm by purchasing land next to it and a couple small blocks that were within the property. We improved it by grading (leveling) the fields and installing an underground pipe system for irrigation purposes. We did some cash crops but ended up stock farming cattle as that was easiest for me to do because of my custom farming for other people.

In late summer of 1947 Ruth's Dad built this house we live in and financed it and we made $40.00 per month payments to him until we paid off $4610. 00

Since then, we built a 20 x 14 living room onto the house and pushed the west wall of the dining room out 9 feet and put in a Franklin fireplace. My Mother and Dad moved in with us in late summer 1979. In a short while, I extended the northeast bedroom which was already 14 x 16. I pushed part of the north wall out by 10 feet and on the west of that, I put a nice bathroom. Really made it nice for them and they enjoyed that very much. We sure could have used that when our kids were coming up but just didn't have the money to do it then.

During all these main events, we had three children. Nancy in March 1949, Rosemary in July 1951, and Edward in August of 1954. Of course, we have grandchildren now and also two great grandchildren.

After high school, the kids all went to college. Nancy attended Howard Payne College and Austin Peay State University; Rosemary attended Uvalde Junior College, Howard Payne College, and Florida Bible College. Ed attended Uvalde Junior College and then went to Texas A&M getting his degree. Nancy married Ron Small, lives in Clarksville, Tennessee, and she is the general manager for a large Real Estate Firm. Rosemary married Larry Stewart, lives in Rockport, Texas and is

24

manager of her house - cook and bottle washer. Ed is the manager of the Underground Water District for this area. He married Katy Albright. When Ed was to be a senior in high school the racial tension was so great we had to put him in school in Carrizo Springs. In order to do that, we had to move into Dimmit County. Charlie Riha fixed up a mobile home and placed it behind his parent's house and we moved into it. I traded Charlie a polled Hereford bull for the use of the mobile home that school year.

My Dad died in November 1980 and my Mother passed away in April 1983. My brother Jim died in April 1992 and his twin brother Harold died in August 1998. That leaves two of us. My brother John who is the oldest at 82 years old and I, the youngest, am past 76 years old.

A ROADRUNNER TALE

One day out at the farm, back in the 50's, I was walking out to the front gate of the yard and I saw a roadrunner fooling around. I picked up a rock about the size of a marble and threw it at him and hit him right on the side of the head. He fell dead as if he had been shot. I picked him up to look at him and as I turned him over he perked up and looked me straight in the eye and "fell dead" again. I was casually holding him, looking at him and all at once in an instant, he was gone! Now I know birds have a brain but this guy used his along with a little strategy.

DOG BAYS SNAKE

I was doing some work for Mr. Bill Gates out east of town. I was bundling hegari feed with a row binder. I was working on my machine which I did quite often, and I heard my little Rat Terrier dog barking at something up the field about seventy-five yards. I walked up to see what she was barking at. She had a big rattlesnake bayed. When I came, she got too excited and got too close to the snake and the snake struck at her hitting her on the head. She shook the snake loose and ran back to the truck. I had brought a spud bar with me so I killed the snake and went to see about my dog. She had gotten up on the seat where she always rode and was just laying there. Her little head was already swelling. I didn't know what to do so I went up to Mr. Gate's house and asked him what I should do. He said he didn't really know but guessed he would put some kerosene on it. I would have gone to a Vet but there was none in this part of the country. I took her home and put the kerosene on her and hoped for the best. Her little head swelled just as round as a ball - her nose was just two little black holes in the ball. In a few days the swelling went down and she became as good as new. I'll tell you one thing, she kept her distance from those snakes after that.

BROKEN SET LINE POLE

Back in the early 40's Jim and I made a trip down the river. The war was on or about to be on and I guess we wanted to have one more fun time before we went to get the war over with. Jim was living in Carrizo managing a store for Keith and Roberts. He and a friend of his had built a boat. I would classify it as a feed trough. The thing was made of 1 x 12 for sides and 2 x 12 for ends. The floor was made of regular flooring - 1 x 4 tongue and groove material. Now, you talk about heavy - it was.

Robert McNeil, Jim and Jack Riggs were coming down too but not until the next day. Jim and I had gotten down to the Evans Lake and had our camp set up and our lines set out when they came the next day. We didn't use motors back in those days - we didn't know what a motor was - at least we had that much less weight in the boat. After they got down there, we'd borrow their boat to run our lines with if they weren't going to be using it for a little while. Robert had built his boat and it was done right. It had a metal bottom so was much lighter because of that and the ends were narrowed and slanted up and was much easier to paddle.

We caught plenty fish. We found a crappie hole and I guess we could have sunk our boat with them. We turned most of the fish back, as we had no way to preserve them. We didn't know what an ice chest was back then. We tried keeping just two or three catfish alive to bring home.

Anyway, the last morning, Jim and I borrowed their boat to go run and take up our lines. Right at the beginning or the head of the lake is a nice hole and there was a pile of logs in the middle of it. They had a pole stuck down in there and a line set. Jim and I decided to pull one on them. We straightened the hook (boy, it was a heavy, very strong hook - we had to use two pairs of pliers to do it) and then broke the pole in the middle and left it that way. We got back to camp and while we were packing up to go on down the river, they went to run their lines. About the time we got packed up to go, they came back and boy, they were telling about the big one that broke their pole and straightened out the hook. Boy, they said tonight they were going to fix him -

they were going to get a bigger pole and better hook and get that sucker.

When we got home I guess we must have told it around because Mrs. McNeil got hold of it; she told them when they got in that we had pulled one on them. Then, they put out the story about getting a big one on that line and it was so big, they turned the boat over when they loaded it in. Of course we didn't bite.

ANOTHER WAY TO HAVE FRESH VENISON

One day my Dad and I were going hunting. We went up to Jess Nash's place. His place was a pretty good ways from ours. We went west on the last crossroad about 8 miles north of Crystal City. This road followed the south border of the 7D ranch about three miles west, and then went north along its west fence. Right there at that corner, there was a locked gate - one of those big ole Frame locks - looked kinda like a railroad lock. Well, we had a bunch of keys and one of these keys opened this lock. From this corner we went north a couple miles and then west again and then north coming to Jess's place. We didn't get a deer that morning. On the way home, coming south along the 7D we saw a nice little buck standing out in the pasture about fifty yards. As we stopped and were backing up, I got out on the running board and put my gun over the top of the car. We couldn't see the deer so we supposed he had run. I got back into the car and as we started off, there he was, still standing there. I got back out on the running board and all I could see was his nose up to his eyes. I cracked down on him and he reared up and fell backwards. I jumped over the fence and hurriedly dragged him to the car. He was bleeding like crazy, but we crammed him into the trunk and took off. We hadn't gone far when he began kicking and pretty soon the back of the seat began coming out. I jumped back there and pushed it back the best I could. He was still raising cane when we got to the locked gate, so Dad had to get out and open the gate, drive through it, then get back out to close and lock the gate.

When we got out on the highway, I reached back in there to see if I could tell if the deer was dead or not. The road was so bumpy I couldn't tell so I just stayed in the back seat just in case. He wasn't kicking anymore so I figured he had bled to death.

When we got back to the farm, we drove down to the pump to dress the deer. We both got out of the car and if it had been me, I would have opened the trunk lid wide open. But Dad opened it just a little and that deer came unglued again. He couldn't close the lid because the deer had gotten one leg out and then he was kicking the seat out again, so I jumped back in the car to hold the seat from coming out. There we were, wondering what in the world we were going to do. Granddad's house was about two hundred yards up on the hill. He was pretty deaf and I figured I couldn't make him hear me, but I had no choice but to try. I hollered and whistled and believe it or not, he answered me fairly soon, "What you want?" I told him to bring a rope quick. He did. I took the rope and went around the deer a couple times and tied it the best I could. I kept the rope tight as I got out of the car. Granddad handed Dad's gun to him. Dad opened the trunk lid wide open and the deer sprang out of that trunk like a jack in the box. Somehow, the rope had about three feet of slack in it, but did hold. Dad went to shoot the deer and didn't have a bullet in his gun and the deer wasn't wanting to hang around but Dad got a bullet in the gun and settled the matter pretty quick.

WRONG KIND OF FISH BAIT

One time Frank Rutledge and I were going fishing down on the Habernig place that his dad had. The place had lakefront so we took a boat or maybe they had one there. We figured we could shoot some rabbits to use for fish bait but there wasn't a rabbit to be seen. Finally we saw an old yellow tomcat and we killed him. First of all, skinning an old tomcat is not a pretty good thing to do. Anyway, we got the thing skinned and cut up for bait. The next morning we went to take the fish off the lines and found out all we took off was the bait we had put on. I don't remember a single bait being gone. You'd think turtles and gars would eat that stuff but they didn't.

On another occasion Frank and I went up the river from the Ray place. We went all the way to the Butler Hole. That was in the days before the upper Nueces Dam was there so there was no backwater. We fought logjams by the plenty. One good thing about it, we didn't travel as heavy then as we do now. No ice chest, no water buckets, no bedding other than a small tarp and a couple fishing poles and some set lines or trotlines. I had my little Fox Terrier dog with me this time. We were going to be gone only three days. For food, we decided to take a bunch of eggs and that's all. We threw in a tin can to boil the eggs in so actually we didn't have much weight in the boat. Any way you look at it, it was a long hard pull. Well, you know, boiled eggs are pretty good (I don't mind eating a couple even now) but trying to make three meals a day on them gets a little much pretty quick. Even the dog refused them about the second day. We didn't even take a frying pan or anything else. We traveled light.

I've heard about loosing weight on boiled egg diets. If you happen to know Frank Rutledge ask him if he ever went camping and was going to live on boiled eggs. Don't tell him that I sent you.

TRAVELING SNAKE

My Granddad had a 1926 Chevrolet turtleback, one-seated car with a soft top. The garage he kept it in was no more than a couple feet longer and a couple feet wider than the car. The garage had a 2 x 4 plate around the bottom one around the top and one around the middle. The sides were 1x10's placed up and down. It had a tin roof nailed to rafters about four feet apart that ran long ways with the garage and it had a floor in it. It had doors too, but I never saw them when they were closed.

Anyway, the story is; to get into the car, you had to squeeze between the car and the wall and there were always wasp nests under that middle plate. Granddad always said, "Don't bother them and they won't bother you." It kept us kids from getting in his car I tell you for sure. And then, he had a snake that lived in the car. He always said not to bother his snake; that it won't hurt a thing. He said the snake went to town with him most of the time. The good part I guess, it was a bull snake and he had a good place to live in out of the weather and I'm sure he could catch plenty mice under the seat there. I guess like the saying goes, "everyone to his own liking."

FIRST TIME OVERSEAS

By the title, one might surmise that I was in the service. Yes, you are right. I was called into Uncle Sam's gathering of friends during World War II. I was sent to Shepherd Field, Texas for my military basic training. From there I was sent to Scott Field, Illinois. Here I trained to be a high-speed radio operator. This may sound peculiar but what it meant was, receiving and sending International Morse code efficiently at the speed of 25 words per minute or more.

When this training was complete a bunch of us were shipped to Will Rogers Field at Oklahoma City. There, they said we were going to be screened and processed for overseas shipment. I was there some weeks and then sent to Shepherd Field, Texas. Why I was sent to these places after I had completed my training is beyond me. I guess it was just the military way. From Texas, I was shipped to Presque Isle, Maine for overseas shipment.

I feel you should know about this little trip - from Texas to Maine. It was hot summer time in Texas when we left - in fact, it was the day before payday - no pay till later. Didn't need it anyway - couldn't get off the train to spend it. The time of year was the day before the last day of May. I boarded this troop train along with many others and away we rolled north. The train took us through Chicago, Albany, New York, and Bangor, Maine and to Presque Isle, Maine.

We were in route about nine days. When we reached Chicago, it began cooling off at night and finally cold and colder. Just want you to remember that we were in summer uniform and I don't remember there being any heat on that troop train. The train stopped a little while in Bangor and I remember a woman sticking her head out of her house, which wasn't too far from the tracks and asked, "You going over or coming back?" We said we were going to Presque Isle and she said, "Oh, you don't want to go up there, it snowed up there last night." Sure enough, when we got there, the ground was covered with snow.

The drivers of the shuttle buses had their OD uniforms on and their overcoats on. Now, you can guess how we felt - leaving a hot country and arriving in a cold one. Something like stepping out of a 98-degree room and into a 29-degree room. We were, as I said before, in summer uniform with not even a field jacket. This was one case where the military's intelligence system didn't function very well. Maybe this wasn't the trouble - maybe it was the thoughtlessness of the officers in charge of the shipment. Anyway, we were as cold as a well digger's tail in Montana and didn't get our winter clothes until we were assigned to and settled in our quarters.

We were there about a week and got processed some more and then placed on an alert. When on an alert, you had to have your duffel packed and ready to grab and run at any moment. You were not allowed to go off base. There were about three places we could go to. We could go to the cantina, mess hall, and the movies. When we left our quarters, we had to sign out and state where we were going to be. I think it was two evenings all of us signed out to go to the movies. This last evening, there was this guy by the name of John Spain. He said he didn't feel very well and he was going to stay in quarters. Well, the rest of us just got seated in the theater and an announcement came over the loud speakers for our alert to report to our quarters right away. Well, we did and grabbed our duffel and were on a shuttle bus headed for the airfield. Only thing, Mr. Spain wasn't with us.

They shuttled us right up to a B-17 bomber and we crawled in that thing and were rolling out to the runway pretty quick. We got airborne and were off into the wild blue yonder and had no idea where we were going. It seems like it was about ten o'clock or so when we sat down. They marched us to a mess hall and fed us a meal. We asked some one in there where we were and they told us we were in Stephenville, Newfoundland. I suppose the plane was serviced while we ate. In a short while we were back on the plane and off again. It seemed to get daylight pretty quick so I figured we were flying east. Looking out a window, I could see the white caps on the water and then I noticed the wing tip. It seemed to be flopping up and down an awful lot and I thought sure, the wing was breaking off. I learned a lot of stuff about planes after that.

About 14 hours after leaving Newfoundland, we sat down on the ground once more. The pilot stepped back where we were and he asked, "You guys worried?" We said "no", and he wiped his brow and said that he had been very worried. Said he'd been circling this place for two hours and couldn't find it. Well, the 24 of us (should have been 25) got off the plane into shuttle buses and took off to somewhere. I asked the driver if that was a mountain or a black cloud that I could see over there through a break in the fog. He said he didn't know, he'd been there two weeks and hadn't been able to see that far yet. I guess it was no wonder the pilot couldn't find the place.

After we were assigned to our quarters, we found out that we were on the island of Santa Maria, Azores. We also found out that fog was a big problem there.

The next day or so here comes John Spain - remember him? That evening we all went to the show and he was going to stay in - well, a little while after we had gone to the show, he decided to go to the canteen and get himself a milk shake. When he returned to quarters, everybody's stuff was gone. Boy, he was some kind of glad to see us. You'd thought that we had been bosom buddies all our lives.

Spain said that the next morning, they called him up on the carpet in front of high brass and by the way they started questioning him; he didn't know what might happen. They told him that he could be charged with desertion and that was a very serious charge. He said he finally got himself together enough and told the officer that he had signed out on the roster and didn't think he was doing anything wrong. The officer wanted to see the roster and when he saw Spain had signed out, the officer told the sergeant to get that CQ in here. Really, it was the CQ's fault because he failed to see that Spain had signed out to go to the canteen. Well, it got Spain off the hook and they put him on a plane coming our way. He said that sure was a lonesome 18 hours. Said he was back in the belly of that big thing all by himself. The plane had a load of lettuce in it. I can see why he was glad to see someone whom he knew.

They told us we were now ready to go to work. We were assigned to an Air to Ground position along side an experienced operator. At first, it was really difficult because there was so much static and interference on the air. We had done all this in training but we used oscillators and there was no static at all and on radio nets using low power transmitters there was very little static and no interference. At first, I said to myself, I'll never get this. After two or three days, you'd begin to pick out a little and learn how the different signals sounded. After you begin picking out those signals it became interesting. At first, I was nervous when I sent a signal knowing I was being heard for thousands of miles around. In about two weeks I was able to do the job well enough to be considered a high-speed operator. Our MOS numbers were 760 and 760D. The 760 was an Air to Ground operator and the 760D meant that we also were Direction Finder operators. International Morse Code was our means of communicating. I suppose learning code is about like learning a language and when you can do it, you enjoy it.

WANTED TO GET MARRIED IN 1945 BUT DIDN'T DO IT UNTIL 1946

Back in 1945 I got back to the states and after being overseas you automatically got a furlough. I flew into an airfield in New Hampshire in the middle of the night. I managed to get my leave papers right away and caught a train over to Boston. There I had to change depots and I had no idea where the other one was so I hailed a cab. He took me there right away. I took a train from Boston to St Louis. Seems like the schedule stated 30 some hours but because of the icy weather, it took us an extra 36 hours. They said we were ice bound. I could see in places that they had to build fires under the switches to thaw them in order to switch the train from one track to another. The time of year was 3 or 4 days before Christmas and I was supposed to be home for Christmas.

When I arrived in St Louis I found the depot very crowded. I guess during the war about the only public travel facilities was by train or bus. I'd been in some of those bus stations too and they were packed. People didn't drive a whole lot because of gasoline rationing. Boy, when I went to board the train in St. Louis, you talk about being crowed. That thing filled up very quickly. The G.I. had priority over the civilians but it was still crowded. There was quite a bunch of people including me that didn't get inside the coach. There is a vestibule on the end of the car and we were standing in it. The conductor told us we couldn't ride there that we would freeze to death - nobody moved. He kept telling us we could not ride there - you'll freeze to death. Still, nobody moved. Finally they put on an old coach and the overflow got in it. The thing didn't have any heat in it and I thought I'd freeze in it. We wouldn't have gotten outa town trying to ride on that vestibule. We'd been like cordwood.

When we arrived in Little Rock, Arkansas, I got a chance to get to a telephone and call the Roberts and asked them to get word to Mother and Dad that I would be in San Antonio at a prescribed time the next evening. When the train pulled in to the depot and I got off, there they were. My brothers, John and Harold, Benard (Jim's future wife) and my girl, Ruth, were right there waiting for me.

This was Christmas Eve so Ruth and I didn't get much time together because she had to go back to Temple on Christmas day to resume her M.T. training at Scott and White the day after. We had about 3 hours together on the way home (speed limit you remember was 35 MPH in those war days) and then a little time when I took her home from the farm. It didn't take us long to figure out what we were going to do. I was coming to Temple in three days and we'd see about getting our marriage license and she would see about getting 30 days leave from training and with that done, we'd go down to Jourdanton and get Bro. Burnie to marry us.

When I went up it must have been close to a weekend. We went up to Ft. Worth to see Benard and Dorothy. The next day when Ruth secured her leave which might have been a Monday and then on our way to Jourdanton we stopped at Belton (county seat) to get our marriage licenses and then we went on down to Jourdanton.

We arrived Jourdanton in late afternoon and guess what, no preacher. My mother had written him a note telling him that we were coming but I guess she didn't say what day. He lived in a hotel and the attendant said he thought Bro. Burnie would be in before too long - if he was going to stay away, he always told them or left word at the desk. Well, while we waited, we went over to Pleasanton a few miles away to see some people I knew. While visiting the Bryants somehow we met their pastor and he offered to marry us. We said thanks but we wanted Bro. Burnie to do it. As a matter of fact, when we bought our licenses in Belton that afternoon, the clerk told us that there was a J.P.'s office next door- he'd be glad to marry us.

We went back over to the hotel but Bro. Burnie still hadn't come in. It was bedtime now so I got a room for Ruth and I asked the hotel clerk if I could stay in Bro. Burnie's room and he said I could.

Ok, next morning we decided to go back over to Pleasanton and get that preacher to marry us. Well, guess what, he had gotten called out of town to a sick sister. We even began considering a Justice of the Peace by now but, this was New

39

Years Day, 1946. Being a holiday, we figured all the offices would be closed so we decided to go back to Jourdanton and see if they had heard any thing from Bro. Burnie. They hadn't heard from him. Then we decided to go over to the church and low and behold, he was there. They were doing some remodeling on the building and he had been in San Antonio the day before and had stayed with friends that night. He said he had gotten my mother's card but some how the way he read it, he thought we were coming the next day. I guess by now, he saw the urgency. After all, he had already delayed us a year. We had done our dead level best to get married in 1945 but it was in 1946 before it happened.

He took us down to the hotel lobby and performed the ceremony. After the ceremony he fixed up the papers and we bid him adios (good bye) and we went back to Pleasanton for New Year's dinner with the Bryants.

After dinner we went into San Antonio for a few days. When we returned home, we stayed with Ruth's folks a while and then with my folks.

One day, we went up on the river hunting. Andy Majek and his wife came out and went with us. I don't know that we were really trying to kill any game. However, Ruth did bag an armadillo. I've got a picture of the great white hunter to prove it.

Our 30-day leaves were coming to a quick end. All too soon it was time to go. Ruth's Dad took us over to Dilley to catch the train. Ruth got off at Temple and I went on to Chicopee Falls, Massachusetts and reported to Westover Field.

At Westover Field I reported to a Captain Hardy. The Captain was a WAC and she told me that I was up for discharge. I told her "No Ma'am, I don't think so but it would suit me all right." After looking through more papers, she said, "No, you're supposed to go back overseas." I told her I was sure of that. I asked her if she had any papers on a Sgt. Vance High. She looked and said "Yes I do, he got an extension on his leave and will be in here day after tomorrow." I asked her if I could wait for him. We had come from overseas together and sure would like to get back together. She accommodated me and assigned me to a transit barracks. She had told me that Vance had gotten an extension on his leave and I thought to myself, I put in for one also and I didn't get one.

All I remembered about Westover Field was a nice WAC and it snowed so hard that you couldn't see across the street. I lay in that transit barracks until Vance came. He had reported to the Captain too and she told him to come over and get me and come back to her office. She was fixing to ship us right out over the pond again when Vance asked her if it would be possible for us to visit New York City before going back overseas. She said sure, she'd transfer us over to Fort Totten out on Long Island. Ok, we took the train heading for Grand Central Station, New York. When we got in there we walked up five floors and they were big floors too because those trains are tall. We were supposed to report out to LaGuardia Field. But, instead we went on Fifth Avenue and got a hotel room. We messed around New York two days before reporting at LaGuardia Field. Vance was one of these guys that had to see a lot of stuff that I didn't care about. We had to go in the Waldorf Astoria Hotel, and another hot tamale hotel that I can't think of the name of. We went up the Empire State Building and that, I enjoyed.

After a couple days of sight seeing we reported out to LaGuardia Field and were shuttled out to Fort Totten.

When we got to Fort Totten we were assigned to a transit barracks. No one asked us why we were late or anything. Next morning pretty early an announcement came over the loud speaker for all embarkees to fall out for roll call and detail. Well, we thought we were debarkees (departing) so we didn't bother to fall out for the roll call. It caught up with us later on, however.

Somehow, Vance got hold of a book of passes that had been stamped with some officer's signature and we were going in town every afternoon. We went to at least two theaters every time we went. Vance seemed to think he was in heaven when he was able to see any of the movie stars in person. All these theaters had stage shows with "live" stars in between each showing of the film. To me it was just so much baloney. Attending these shows didn't cost us much - we GIs had to pay only $.50 cents for our tickets.

41

After a few days of this extravagance Vance ran out of money. He called his dad and asked for some money and he said that he would send him some via Western Union. Ok, we went to the Western Union office on the Fort and they told Vance that he would have to pick up any message or money at his Orderly Room. Ok, we went to the Orderly Room. I sat outside while he went in to get his money. In a little while, Vance came out and said "Boy, we are in trouble - bad." I asked why so and he said we have been marked AWOL (away with out leave) for a week. He said the Warrant Officer (commanding officer in this case) asked him if he knew anything about this Sgt. Walker. Vance told him yes, he was waiting outside. He told Vance to "GO GET HIM." Well, to say the least, we got a little lesson in education right then. We explained that we thought "debarking" meant "going over" and he let us know that ignorance of the law is no excuse. The law reads that this could be considered desertion and desertion could be punished by using bullets. Well, praise the Lord that God works in miraculous and mysterious ways. He gave us a good talking to and told us he was putting us in charge of the roll call and detail assignment because we were the highest-ranking NonComs in the transit area right now. Oh boy, we had a job now. It turned out though that we had to do it only once. We got our shipping orders that day and we were gone the next day.

On our way to Newfoundland Vance suggested that we try to get stationed there. It really didn't make any difference to me so I said ok with me. Well when we arrived Stephenville, Newfoundland we asked to be stationed there. We got it all right but Vance got assigned to Headquarters and I got the Working Detachment. His was an inside job and mine was "a get out in any kind of weather no matter what" job. That's the kind of job I always had but it wasn't cold, icy and miserable, only wet. It didn't take long until I wished I was back in the Azores.

Just a short while, a matter of a week or less, I was visiting with a friend whom I had known in the Azores and we were telling each other how we wished we were back down there. I don't know how it happened but all at once there stood our Commanding Officer, Lt. Ricky from the Azores. Bob Wells and I were visiting with our old C.O. and we mentioned that we'd like to be back down in the islands. Lt. Ricky asked if we really meant that. "Yes Sir, we really do." He told us to go pack our bags - he really needed us down there. The Base on Santa Maria, Azores was being phased out but they had taken too many men away too quick making the men left to have to double up too much. I guess our C.O. knew what he was doing when he told us to pack up - we were on our way that night.

Months later the C.O. said something about not being able to get any promotions in rank for his men. He said he was going up to headquarters and he was going to find out where all the rank was being handed out. Bob and I watched the bulletin board and sure enough, our names appeared there - we both were promoted to Staff Sgt. Bob and I were down at our Squadron Headquarters when the C.O. came in and he asked us did we see what he had done for us. Did we see? We already had our stripes sewed on. He said they were giving out all the allotted rank to the guys up there in Wing Headquarters. Thank you Sir.

MOUSE IN THE BOX

Back in 1947 Ruth and I were living a couple miles out in the country. We rented an apartment from the Harold's. It was part of their house that they had closed off and made an apartment out of. It's the house where Hal and Jean Stalling live now and have been for years.

One morning Ruth went in the kitchen to fix breakfast. She took the Malto Meal box off the shelf. She said there seemed to be something alive in the box and about that time, a little mouse jumped up out of the box. As she slung the box and hollered, all at the same time, the mouse fell to the floor. As she started to run, she stepped on the mouse smearing him real good.

Well, Mrs. Harold heard the scream and it must have been a good one - she rushed in to see what I was doing to Ruth.

WATER SOFTENER THAT DIDN'T WORK

I got out of the service in late 1946 and I went to Temple, Texas where Ruth was about to finish her Lab training. After she finished, we came home. The first of 1947 she went to work for Dr. Poindexter here at the Crystal Clinic and Hospital. I thought that I didn't want to farm for a living so I ventured into the business world.

I bought a service station down in the middle of town and sat back and waited for the money to roll in. Well, I didn't do so pretty good and before long I decided to sell to some other sucker. About the only money I made was fixing flats. Doing that didn't cost much. Plenty of hard work though.

It took nearly a year before a buyer by the name of J. D. Web came along who needed to get rich in the station business. J. D. had a wife, two young boys, a sister, and a father. It was in the first part of 1948 when he bought me out.

They were nice folks and we visited back and forth a good bit. The sister was an old maid schoolteacher.

In the summer of '48, Ruth's Dad went out to Alpine to up grade himself and get higher degrees in his education. We decided to go out to Carlsbad Caverns that summer. We took Ruth's mom and brothers and invited Miss Web to go. We had a car full when we got loaded up, but the old Buick made the pull.

We dropped off Mama Bill and the boys at Alpine and we and Miss Web headed on to Carlsbad. We went up through Pecos and into New Mexico. Just a few miles to the first little town in New Mexico, there was a dirt road going through to White City. There were several roads taking off from that one and they weren't marked very well so we were always in doubt if we were on the right road or not. It was getting late when we came to a resort on the Black River. We stopped for directions and the man invited us in to eat. Said they were serving a family style meal. We accepted and enjoyed the meal very much. Afterwards, they invited us to stay the night. They told us the Caverns didn't open until 9 A.M. and it wasn't all that far over there. Ok, we took a duplex and would have breakfast with them next morning and then we'd be on our way.

We shared the duplex with Miss Web and we had to share the bath. I went in to bathe first and found that the water was very hard and I think I wore out two or three bars of soap trying to get a lather. After I bathed, Ruth went in and she found the water to be very hard too. There on the tub where the water valves were, she saw this one with an "S" on it and thought maybe that meant "softener." She pushed that thing and she said she noticed the water quit running and then about that time, the water came out of the showerhead and scared the dickens out of her. She screamed real loud when the water hit her. I ran in to see what in the world had happened and so did Miss Web. I told her that "S" meant shower and she said that she noticed the water quit running but didn't know why. She wasn't used to that sort of thing.

Things turned out all right. Next day we went on to the caverns and did the tour. Going back to Alpine we went a little farther west. We saw the highest point in Texas, El Capitan. We went down through the Salt Flat country. There was a number of "Dust Devils" working out in that country. I think there was a place called Wink out in there somewhere. At a distance, those Dust Devils appeared to be standing still. After driving a few miles, we came to one right in the road and like a dummy I drove right into it. I tell you what, before we got through that thing, I wished I hadn't been so smart. It pitched us around right smart. I believe if we'd been in a little light car, we might have been stacked.

The rest of our trip went fine. We picked up Ruth's mother and brothers and headed back to Crystal City.

BALED RATTLESNAKES

This story took place on the Rubyola farm some ten miles east of town. Potter Alger was living on the place and farming it. He had fifty acres of red top cane and engaged me to cut and bale it. This cane was very heavy so it took quite a long time for it to dry enough to bale it. Sometimes it took up to two weeks laying in the hot sun to be dry enough. This was before the day of the hay conditioner or crimper. Had I had one of those, the drying time would have been cut to about a third.

When I did start I would rake only what I could bale that day. After baling a day or so, Potter started hauling and stacking his hay. The next day, he came to me and told me that I sure was getting a lot of rattlesnakes in the bales. I found that hard to believe because I had not seen a single snake.

I started watching the men that were loading the hay and every little bit, I'd see them hitting something with a chain. Those snakes were under the windrow and the ones that didn't go into the machine, crawled either under the next windrow or got under a bale of hay. Kenneth, Ruth's oldest brother was helping me. His main job was to straighten out the big wads of hay that the side delivery rake would leave sometimes. He hadn't seen any snakes either so I told him to walk behind the baler. Sure enough, he started seeing snakes - plenty of them. Just like I had figured, the ones that didn't go into the baler, crawled under the next windrow or under a bale. I began watching closer as the windrow was picked up and going into the baler and I began seeing snakes too.

We'd try killing those snakes by running the pitchfork tine through their head. That didn't do too well. Their little skull was about the size of a BB and the tine would slip off it. We tried putting their heads up against the exhaust pipe on the baler's engine. Boy, that would kill them all right, but when holding the head against that hot pipe, their mouth would open wide and the fangs popped out and the venom would spurt. Well, we couldn't have that. To get venom all over the machinery would be very hazardous. So we dispensed with that idea. I really don't remember what we did about the snakes -

just left them I guess.

I know one thing; Kenneth quit working those piles and I didn't blame him a bit. But then, guess who got to do it? I would have quit too but I couldn't - just became much more observant and hoped for the best.

MEAT ARRIVES LATE

Back in '48 or '49 I was attending an Ag School and we were going to throw a Bar-B-Q. Edwin Hamilton was living on the Worm farm and he said he'd furnish the meat. He asked me to come out and help him get a couple nice young deer. I went out and we went hunting that night and we couldn't see a deer much less kill one. Along about the middle of the night we decided to go road hunting and I guess we drove all over three counties and still came up empty handed.

There was a farmer south of the McNeil place who had goats so we decided to go out there and buy some young goats. We did but by the time we got them bought, cleaned and to the guy that was going to do the Bar-B-Q'n, it was well after 9 o'clock in the morning and he had told us he had to have the meat by six in the morning. Orville Bookout was doing the cooking and to say the least, he was upset. He got the meat right on but you know how things like that turn out. The meal was served an hour and a half late and the meat burned on the outside and raw on the inside. Of course it was Edwin's and my fault and sure enough it was. It took us a while to live that one down.

ANOTHER WAY FOR TURKEY

One time my Granddad was fishing down on the river.
When he got ready to go to the house, he leaned his fishing pole
up against a tree. Later that afternoon he came back to fish some
more. When he got there, what do you think he had on his line?
He had left the bait on and a turkey grabbed it and got caught.
He said it wasn't fish but it worked all right. He said you might
call this one a Ripley, "believe it or not" thing. Said it sure did
happen though.

DODGING ONE STORM AND GOING INTO ANOTHER

In the summer of 1948 my Uncle Lester came from Cheyenne, Wyoming to visit. He then took my Granddad back with him - taking him to North Platte, Nebraska to visit his daughter (my Aunt Gladys) first for a couple weeks and then he went back and got him and took him up to Cheyenne. After he visited there a while, I was to go and get him. He had bought a 1940 Chevrolet from Nick Roberts and I was going in it.

I was attending an Ag School so I had to time my trip to fit in with that schedule. I attended class one evening and left right after class. I drove up highway 83 all the way to North Platte. North of Leakey the road turned east and went to Mountain Home and to Junction. When I was going north from Leakey, I was heading right into a cloud that had lots of lightening in it. When I went to Mountain Home and then back to Junction, I went around that cloud just as pretty as you please. From Junction the road pretty well went north again. I was getting up close to Abilene and there was another bad looking cloud. I didn't get to go around this one - it showered down on me as I was going through Abilene and of course in those days, you had to go right through the towns (no by-passes) and it was raining so hard that I had trouble seeing the signs.

After I got out of the rain and saw that I was on the right road, I began to get sleepy. I guess it was 2 or 3 in the morning when I decided to pull off the road and sleep a little. I pulled off the road and I realized I was in mud. That kinda woke me up and I thought I'd better see if I was stuck or not. It took a little doings but I got back on the road and then I wasn't sleepy any more. I stopped at the next cafe that was open and got a cup of coffee and I never got sleepy again. Oh yeah, I gassed up often because I didn't wanta run out of gas.

When I got to McCook, Nebraska I looked up some kinfolk whom I had never seen. Uncle Lester had stopped there with Granddad and they wanted to see some of his folk so I went by. I got there around 2 in the afternoon and just at the right time. This lady was taking bread out of the oven. Boy - some good -

just like Mom's at home. I visited there for an hour or so and headed on to North Platte. I guess I got up there between 5 and 6 o'clock P.M.

I stayed at Aunt Gladys' three days, I think it was. My cousin Bob took me fishing. The lines they set are lines attached to jugs with an anchor on the bottom and then put the hooks up the line. I guess one of the thrills is looking for the jugs the next morning and wondering what moved it. There were no trees to tie lines to. All my life, I always thought there were trees along the banks for that purpose. Of course I had never been out of Zavala County. I don't know if we found all the jugs or not but we did make headlines in a North Platte Paper. We had gotten one cat fish that weighed 11 pounds. They acted like that was a trophy.

I had spent my allotted time in North Platte and it was time to go to Cheyenne. Cheyenne is 200 miles west - I followed the Lincoln Highway number 30 all the way. Now, you would follow I-80. On my way that day, I was heading straight into a "dark black cloud." I was beginning to get under it and all of a sudden, the thing turned white. Of course I slowed considerably thinking I was going to hit hard rain. It was hail; small "pea" size and plenty of it. The ground turned white real quick and in places where the wind blew, it drifted into banks. I sat still until it let up and then with 3 inches of hail on the road; I didn't go very fast. Finally arriving in Cheyenne and finding my Uncle's house I was ready for a little rest.

I visited my folks in Cheyenne a couple days and then my Granddad and I left heading south. We stopped in Denver, Colorado to visit a cousin who was attending some sort of school there. We visited about an hour I guess and went on our way. We stopped down the line to get gas and rest a few minutes. Remember that 1948 was before the day of Interstate highways and the roads took you through every little town. We proceeded on from the station a short ways when I noticed the ampmeter on the dash was reading a slight discharge. I stopped and turned around and went back to the station to get a fan belt. I installed it and we proceeded on. My Granddad asked me how I knew the fan belt had broken. I told him that I noticed the ampmeter didn't show any charge so I knew the generator wasn't turning and that indicated to me that the fan belt was broken. He said "Oh."

We went to White City, New Mexico and took a motel. The next day we toured Carlsbad Caverns - we wanted to see what kind of hole they had in the ground over there. We found out it was a pretty big hole and it took us several hours to walk down in it and get out. I guess we rode an elevator up out of it.

After leaving Carlsbad, New Mexico and entering Texas, we went to a lake that's on the Pecos River - the Dam is called Red Bluff so maybe the lake is Red Bluff Lake. Anyway the old country around there is reddish looking and I suppose that's where it got its name.

From there, I pointed that 1940 Chevy toward Crystal City and it seemed to know the way.

PUT ONE CLUTCH IN RIGHT AFTER ANOTHER

In 1948 my Granddad bought a 1940 Chevrolet from Nick Roberts. It was a pretty nice car; it was black and had four doors. Well, it wasn't too long until the clutch went out. I put one in for him. I'd had a little practice putting clutches in his old 1926 Chevy. Before it was all over with, I learned the clutch replacement business pretty well. This 1940 Chevy had the shift on the steering column and I don't think he ever really learned which gear was which. Course he had to get reverse to get out of his carport but it took him several stabs to find it. When he went to go forward, it didn't matter if he had it in first, second or third (three speed transmission) he would rev the engine to a loud roar and slide the clutch out to where he could feel it wanting to go and then stomp the gas peddle to the floor and slowly it would begin to go. If the clutch wasn't burned out by this time - about a quarter of a mile, he'd start looking for high hole. He might have already had it in high (third gear) but it didn't make any difference. Oh too, I've always thought that a motor should be warmed up before pouring the coal to it - not so - he would get in that car on a cold, cold day to start it. He put the pedal to the floor and when it started, it was turning at least 4000 RPM instantly.

After burning out the third clutch in his car, I told him that the thing was worn out and couldn't be fixed any more. Well, after about two weeks, he asked me if I was going to fix that car for him. If I wasn't, he was going to call Jack Eubanks Chevrolet Company and have them come get it and fix it. OK, that would cost him big bucks so I fixed it again. The day I fixed it, he was ready and dressed to go to town just as soon as I got done. I proceeded to give him a lesson on how to start off and he said, "sure, sure, he knew about that." Well, he got in the car and started it up "his way and started off his way" and he got no more than 300 yards from the house. The whole area around there including the river bottom smelled like rotten eggs. Smoke was coming out of the car. If there had been a collection of grease and dirt it surely would have caught on fire - he had that thing so hot. He walked back to the house where I was standing and told me that something was wrong with his car. It stopped on him. I asked him how long it had been since I put a clutch in it for him. He thought for a second and said, "I don't believe you have ever put a clutch in that car." It was kinda funny (thinking about it now anyway) when the car wouldn't go and I guess he was trying shifting into different gears or anything else he thought might make it go and revving the engine to a high pitch scream making a B-17 Flying Fortress Bomber sound quiet. I must have fixed it for him one more time and I'll bring that up a little later.

Years earlier he would go to town only on Saturdays to get his mail and buy groceries. Later, he got to going to the Saturday afternoon show but would always get home before dark. Then after he got the 1940 Chevy he started going to town at night once in a while. In between clutch burnouts I guess. The last time he went to town and the last time he drove; he went in at night and went to the show. He evidently couldn't find his car and went fooling around town and about three in the morning he went into Ben Achley's house just north of where the Dairy Kream is now. Achley called the law and when they came, they knew who he was and took him over to my brother's house on the west side of town. Jim took him out to the farm and got Dad and they took him down to his house and put him to bed at 4:30 in the morning. Dad went back down there at 7:00 and he was up fixing his breakfast. Dad asked him where he had been the night before and he said, "Right here in bed." Dad had gone back to town with Jim and brought his car home. This time, Dad kept the keys. I asked Granddad two or three weeks later how his car was doing and he said, "It'd do just fine if your dad would let me have the keys."

A SPIKE BUCK JUMPS OUT OF THE TRUCK

When Dad and I were farming oat calves together, sometimes we thought we might run short on water so we would irrigate day and night. This was back in the days when we used ditches and you had to stay with the water. Dad was irrigating during the days and I was doing the night shift.

A time or two during this time of night work, I would have a little time to sleep. A time or two, I would drive over across the highway about a half-mile or so and turn around in the road letting my headlights shine in a field to the south. Most of the time there would be deer feeding there and sometimes they would be close enough to see them pretty good. It was fun looking at them.

After we had finished that round of irrigating, Mother was having us and my brother Jim and his wife out for supper. Jim and Benard had come to our house to pick us up and ride out with them. I wasn't ready to go yet, so Ruth and Benard went on out and Jim and I were coming later, after I bathed.

On the way out, I was telling Jim about seeing those deer over across the highway and he suggested we go look now on our way to the farm. It was good dark by now so things would work good as far as the lights were concerned. Well, we went over there and just as I was slowing down to turn, this spike buck came running to the road. Jim took a shot at him and then he ran back behind up into the dark. I turned around right quick and as I got turned, the deer came out in the road in the lights. Jim took another crack at him and he fell dead. I just supposed he had hit him on the head the way he fell. I drove up beside the deer and we jumped out to load him. I grabbed his long spikes and Jim took hold of his back legs. Just as we got him picked up, he began to kick like everything. Jim said, "What'll we do?" I said, "Throw him in the truck." We threw him in all right and then he began scrambling around and when he got a foothold, he went straight up about ten feet and came down right on top of Jim. Knocked him down and then the deer wobbled up the road in front of the truck, turned around and came back toward the truck and bumped into the truck. Then, he wobbled off to the left, went through the fence and was gone. He stayed gone, too. I could have shot the deer any number of times but I thought he would drop any second. Poor Jim, he got some pretty good scratches on his back and a couple of bruises.

We went on over to Mother's and Dad's for supper. They thought we were pulling their legs when we told them about it but Jim had the marks to prove it.

LEANING THE WRONG WAY

My brother Jim was managing the Western Auto Store for Keith and Roberts here in Crystal City. This story takes place back in the 50's when we didn't know there was an outboard boat motor larger than 3-horse power. Well he got one for stock in the store that was 10-horse power. He couldn't wait to take it out and try it. He had a boat that really wasn't big enough for that size motor but we were going to do it anyway. His boat was 12 feet long and a pointed "V" shape.

Jim called up Perry Payne and me one Sunday afternoon and asked us to go to the lake with him. We put the boat in the Commanche Lake west of town and went for a ride. That 10 horse did a pretty good job with the three of us in it and then Jim wanted to try it alone. He did and it really plowed out of the water and sailed along real good. OK, then I took it out and I really got a thrill out of it. Then it was Perry's time. Perry wasn't really too anxious to do it but we told him to go ahead. He got in the boat and started off and then opened it up. He had gotten about 200 yards from us and out of our sight when we heard it rev up real high and then go "ka - plop". Then we heard someone holler down that way, "He turned it over." By the time we got down the shore to where we could see, Perry was all right and that was the main thing. The way he told us what he did made me think that he never had handled an outboard motor. He said he was going to go to his right so leaned that way and then pulled the handle to him which of course was the wrong thing to do. That threw him right out of the boat and then the boat came up out of the water turned over and "ka - plop" down side up and the motor took in a charge of water and that was it. We were very fortunate no one was hurt.

We got the boat out and loaded up the thing and brought it in to the store. We drained all the water out of it we could and tried to start it. We kept drying the plugs and tried a bunch of times to start it but to no avail. Jim said that he would send it back in and tell them that it was a faulty motor. OK, he sent it back. In a few days, they called him and told him whether he knew it or not, that motor had been dunked and it would cost $90 dollars to fix it. Jim's idea was the three of us had fun with it that day so the three of us could pay for it. So - - we did. Thirty bucks was a lot of money back in them days.

MUD DAUBER WELDING

One day Perry Payne was at the farm in his welding truck. I was with him and we stopped at Granddad's house. He came out and was talking to Perry. I guess he didn't see me or didn't know who I was. I had my hat pulled down over my face a little. Anyway, they got to talking about welding and Granddad told Perry that he had a grandson that welded or thought he did. He makes a weld and when he's through with it, it looks like a mud dauber had done it. (I thought - gee - thanks.) Maybe there was more truth in his statement than I cared to admit.

I first learned to weld a little bit back in 1948 when I was attending an Ag School. In my business of farming and custom farming knowing how to weld was sure an asset.

My first welder was an air craft generator. The biggest problem with it, it had to turn at least 2800 RPM. I purchased a transmission from Bill Brennan at his surplus store. This transmission produced 4 speeds; 1/1, 1/2, 1/3, and 1/4. I put a triple groove pulley of 8 inches driving a smaller pulley on the generator. I hooked the input to a tractor power takeoff. I could get plenty of speed on the generator by turning the tractor about 1200 RPM and the gear box in the 1/3 position. I could put the gearbox in 1/4 and turn the tractor slower but when you struck an arc, it jerked the whole business awfully bad. In the 1/3 position everything went pretty smoothly. This setup was good but you always had to have a tractor there when you welded. Later, I installed a Wisconsin V-4 engine and was able to discard the gearbox and it did not require the use of a tractor. I had it mounted on a little two wheel trailer which made it very handy.

Later on I purchased an old Lincoln 200 amp machine. I had to repair some wires in the exciter and overhauled the engine and made things work pretty good. I put wheels under it and that thing has served me many years. Knowing how to do "mud daubering" has saved me lots of dollars and a lot of time. My welding has held up well - it may not be the prettiest but it has worked. I have welded pipelines of 10-inch diameter pipe and all sorts of repair on my old water lines. I guess you'd call it "general welding."

My Granddad was a blacksmith by trade when he lived in Kansas and when he moved to Texas, he brought his shop with him. Back in the old days before the arc welder or before it was very common, they did what they called forge welding. Two pieces of metal that were going to be welded together had to be heated in the forge and flux put on them to clean them and then at a certain "red hot" temperature the pieces were hammered together. This sort of welding must have been very limited. Nothing could be welded right on the machine. Those boys knew how to do a lot of stuff.

From the old shop I am still using the anvil and the old vice that bolted to a bench and anchored to the floor. I have the forge blower and the cast iron part that the air comes up through where the coal was piled on top of it. When you got the coal burning and then shot the air to it, it would get some H-O-T. I also have several of his old hand tools. I have two draw knives, threading dies, threading taps, reamers, long handled tongs for handling hot pieces of work that were in the forge. I also have a lead loaded billy club that he had taken off a bad guy when he was a lawman in Kansas and my son Ed has a knife that Granddad took off a hard head - this knife was made from a file. Ah, there is a number of things still around such as wrenches and other hand tools that you wouldn't use when we have much better quality tools this day and time.

DUSTY TRICK ON A NEIGHBOR'S WIFE

Perry and Virginia Payne lived behind us facing a side street. I came home from work one day and Perry hollered at me. He knew Ruth wasn't home so he said why didn't I come over and eat supper with them. I said sure but let me go back and clean up first. He said, " OK; say, when you go home, call Virginia on the phone and tell her that you are the telephone maintenance department and you are going to blow out the telephone lines and let's see what she does." Well, I called her and told her. I told her that it could be pretty dusty - she might want to cover things up. The thing that made this really work was that the phone was mounted on the wall up above the dining table and she already had the food on the table. I went back over and Perry and I walked in the house. Virginia had the telephone wrapped up and the food was covered with towels. Perry asked her what in the world was going on. She told us, and of course, it wasn't long until she could tell something haywire was going on. We could hardly talk without laughing and it didn't take long until she knew there was a snake in the grass. We thought we had really pulled one on her. Now, if she would have slid the garbage can over to the table and dumped all the food in it and said, "OK boys, supper's over" you know, I bet we wouldn't have felt so smart. It was funny though, we stood there waiting and Perry asked if we were going to eat. She said, "Yes, sure wish they'd hurry and do it so we could."

I have told this story in her presence a few times and she is always going to shoot me. If this story ever gets published and gets around to her, she may very well shoot me. Ah, she's a good sport though. I - I hope.

A SHOT FROM THE DARK

About the year 1948 I was cutting feed up on the Thoreen place. It was the old Rule place. My grandfather Rule came to this country in 1910 and opened that place up.

I was bundling hegari with a row binder. There was a fellow by the name of Ace Green living on that place. He had a permanent camp, I guess you'd call it. He had electricity though so he had some conveniences. At noon, I would go to his camp and eat my lunch. In visiting with him, he got to telling me about going up the river hunting turkey and deer. I told him that I sure would like to do a little of that. I guess he might have been a little leery to ask me to go with him but later on, he came out in the field and told me if I'd stay up there the next night, we'd go up the river and see what we could do. I told Ruth that night that I was going to stay up there that next night and do a little hunting.

When I quit work that next evening, I took the battery off of my tractor and put in his boat and one of us had a spotlight to take. We motored up to the pipeline crossing (a landmark to any one who used the river much) getting there a little before dark. We sat there and waited for good dark before we proceeded. As we eased up the river we were shining in the trees looking for turkey. It wasn't long before we spotted a turkey high over head. Ace was handling the motor and the light. He asked me if I wanted him to get the turkey with his shotgun. I told him "No, just keep the light on it and be still and I'll get that turkey with my .22." Ok, I did and looking a little more, there were two more in there and I got them. He wanted to know how in the world I did that - I didn't have a light shining down the barrel to see my sights with. I told him I didn't need a light. All I needed was for him to keep the light on the target. I explained how you could do that with a scope. Scopes were relatively new then and he had never used one or maybe never had looked through one. There were a lot of raccoons out that night working in the pecan trees and I shot one or two of them and then he wanted to try. Well, after a few tries, he got to where he could hit one too. Then he wanted to know if maybe he could get a scope put on his .22. I told him I felt sure that Garland Davis (gunsmith) could help him out. I don't think he rested until he got one put on.

A SURPRISE IN THE DARK

Edwin Hamilton was living out on the Worm farm that at one time was part of the Mandell farm - the part that was north of the county road going west. Edwin called me to come out and take a friend of his hunting. This guy was a coach and they called him Cotton.

After dark, Cotton and I walked down in the fields to look for deer. We saw deer all right but never could get up on them close enough for a shot. We spotted a nice buck but he kept his distance. After a while I got tired and sat down to rest. Cotton kept on trying to get up on him and walking him all over the place and in a little bit Cotton's light was shining toward me and once in a while I could see his light shine on the deer. Well, they kept getting closer to me and in a little bit the deer was close enough to me so I took him. We both walked to the deer and he asked me how in the world I did that. He said he never saw me shine my light. I explained to him how you could do this sort of thing when using a scope. This kind of hunting never became legal - it was legal only when you didn't get caught. I'll add this though - everyone who knows me, knows I fib a lot when it comes to "fishing and hunting" stories.

PLANNING AN OUT OF STATE DEER HUNT

In 1958 there was a few of us guys talking about going to the Kaibab National Forest to hunt mule deer. Dr. Henry Daly, Bill Brennan, Dr. John Spencer and I met over at Bill's house to talk about making the hunt. We had read stuff on the Kaibab and the big mule deer bucks that were to be found there. It really sounded great. Someone told us that the Kaibab was overrun with hunters from California and really wouldn't be too smart to go there. Somehow, the thought changed to Colorado.

Somehow when time came closer, Dr. Spencer had to bow out and for what reason, I don't remember. Bill came up with the idea of taking a camp cook. He had talked to Bob Miller, a guy who claimed to have been a cow camp cook. I always thought a cow camp cook had to know how to cook beans and have a coffee pot on at all times. Anyway, Henry and I consented for Bill to engage Mr. Miller to go as our cook.

We set the day for our departure and bright and early Bill was loaded and ready. He and Bob went in his pick-up and Henry and I were going in mine.

Well, you know Henry, (if you don't, you will know him before we get through with all our times hunting together) he had some last minute things to do before we could leave. The main thing was, he decided to take his bow (he was going to play Indian) and he didn't have any broad-head arrows so we looked up Frank Smith and he borrowed some from him. Another last minute thing was a pair of electric socks. He had ordered them a couple days ago and had them sent special quick delivery but it wasn't quick enough. Well, Mary Ann said she would send them up when they came. We had told Bill to go on ahead and we would catch up to him later. We caught up to him about noon, I guess. He was stopped at a service station in Del Rio fueling up. He asked me if I was going to fuel up and I told him no. We found out on this trip that he liked to fuel before his gauge got down to half; he didn't want to take any chances. Later that afternoon he stopped to fuel again and he asked me again if I was going to fuel. I told him "no" and he asked if my truck didn't use gas. What he didn't know was, I had a 67-

gallon propane tank in back and my gas tank full too. That first night we camped a little north of Pecos, Texas so you see how fast we were traveling. The second night, we stayed in Albuquerque, New Mexico with my brother Harold and his wife.

The night we camped north of Pecos, we put up a tent and did a little cooking. We wanted a campfire so we went wood hunting. They have so many sand storms in that country the wood keeps getting covered up deeper and deeper so you have to dig it out.

The next day we made it to Colorado believe it or not. We bought our license in Pagosa Springs and then headed out northwest and went to the Ludwig Ranch. Leslie Brice had told us about this ranch. This ranch was high in the mountains and it's plenty cold there at night. We came to a gate and Henry got out to open it and when he got back in the truck he said, "Man, it's cold out there." We had called from Pagosa Springs and talked with someone at the ranch and they told us to come on out. When we arrived, they were serving a family style meal and they invited us to eat. After we ate, we rented a little cabin for that night. There were two beds in it with mattresses so we had to use our sleeping bags. Next morning there was shooting "around in them hills" and looking out the window, there were people walking in all directions toward the timber. I said then, "You're not about to catch me going out in that timber with all those people out there trying to find something to shoot at." Henry didn't like the idea either.

Henry and I talked to Mr. Ludwig and he said he'd pack us up on the mountain to hunt if we wanted. We went back and talked it over with Bill. He and Bob definitely didn't want to pack in but would be all right if we did. Our big problem was, we had only one set of cookware. We divided that up in such a manner we thought would work and divided the grub. The ranch hands packed our stuff on packhorses and away we went up the trail. It got dark on us pretty quick, and man, did it get cold. I didn't have long handles on and I was about to freeze. Henry said, "Hey, put your hands under the saddle blanket." I want you to know, that helped. We got to this camp about 9 PM. There were hunters there and they were going to be packed out the next morning. They were eating - they were having "pot luck" They said they had put everything in the pot that they had left. They invited us up to eat. They didn't have to ask us twice - we were hungry and very cold and were ready. They had evidently put in a can or two of hot chilies, too, and boy, you talk about hot!

One of those hunters told me that they had all filled out their tags and told me where we could get some elk. We walked out from camp a few yards to where we could see a mountain in the distance and he said, "That's where the elk are." I told him that we were not going to have horses. He said he didn't think we could go that far on foot. I told him I guess we'll just do what we can.

I mentioned the pot luck supper with a lot of hot peppers and it reminds me of the story about the guy who was eating some hot stuff and he was about to burn up. Someone told him to eat some ice cream right quick. The ice cream seemed to do the job all right. Next day he went to the outhouse and pretty soon he started yelling, "Hurry up ice cream, hurry up."

Henry and I didn't put up our tent that night. We laid it on the ground and put our sleeping bags on it and pulled the end of it over us. In the night, we heard the horses that had been hobbled stomping around and Henry got scared that they might run over us. We didn't sleep very well worrying about that.

Next morning the ranch hands packed these hunters out and then we put our tent where theirs was. The little tent I had was 5 x 7 feet and did not have a floor in it. The sleeping bag I had was supposed to keep you warm in sub-O weather but I think you were supposed to be inside a warmed room when that kind of weather came. I just about froze all that week.

We were camped on the edge of Rincon La Oso Creek and between us and the mountain, they showed us where we could find elk near a creek named Rincon La Vaca. The first couple days we didn't venture too far out from camp. I killed a deer and we had plenty meat to eat. The third or fourth day we did get over to that mountain where they told us we could find elk. There was plenty sign there all right but I'm sure you needed to be there at daylight or dusk in the evening. Either time, we would have had to walk in the dark an hour and a half and we were afraid we'd get lost in the dark.

The last day we were there, two hunters on horseback came by our camp a good bit before daylight going up the Rincon La Osa trail. They didn't stop to talk. That evening when Henry and I got back to camp we found the packer who was going to pack us back to the ranch was there and had put up his tent. He had a wood burning heater in his tent so you can guess where Henry and I parked for a while. While we were visiting we heard a noise outside and when we looked, it was those two riders that had come by our camp that morning. They were so cold they couldn't talk. We helped them in to the tent so they could warm up a bit. After a while and a cup of hot coffee they begin to talk a little. One of them was a guide and the other a hunter who had killed a nice buck deer the day before. They had gone to get the deer and this hunter wanted the deer whole so he could have it mounted full. The deer had been hung up and of course it was frozen and they had a terrible time packing it on the packhorse. They had lost it off the packhorse two times and it rolled down steep places and took a lot of time retrieving it and when it lost off again, they just left it. Said they'd try again tomorrow.

Henry and I camped here for a week and we found out that we needed a better sleeping bag or maybe one to go over the ones we had and we sure needed a tent with a floor in it. We had a gas stove and light but we burned our gallon of gas up long before we were to go back to the ranch. Now, we were burning spruce wood (lucky we had taken an ax) and it was about like burning newspapers.

The next morning after the packer came; we packed up and headed toward the ranch. Henry and I fooled around on the way back (they brought us horses to ride back) taking pictures and hoping to see some game. It had gotten cloudy and by the time we got down to the ranch, it was snowing. At the ranch, they told us that today was the time we should have been going up to hunt. A good cover of snow makes good hunting. The game start moving down if it snows much in the high country. All their food gets covered with snow and they go down to where it hasn't snowed. Had we been up there and it snowed a lot, it

69

would have caved our tent down and we would have been in a pickle.

When we got to the ranch we found Bill griping about Bob's cooking and Bob was griping about the wood he had to use to cook with. He was using aspen wood and it did make coals for a little while. We told him that he ought to use some spruce – it burned like paper and he would have something to gripe about.

Bill had killed a deer and had taken it in to Pagosa Springs to put it in storage. He had kept the heart and liver and Bob had made a pot of eggplant and liver stew. Henry didn't like either one so he had a bad time eating any of it.

Next day we packed up and headed for home. We stopped in Pagosa to get Bill's deer. He bought a bunch of dry ice and packed it in the deer and away we went.

Henry and I had told each other how stupid we were to go up on the mountain and freeze for a week and after getting warmed up good in the truck, we started talking about what we were going to do next time.

We got down to Pecos, Texas for the next night. We decided to go to a restaurant and get a meal and then we'd find a camping spot. We finally found a nice looking place and as we started in, we noticed several people in there and they were dressed nice. Bill said that they may not serve us looking like we do and not smelling so good either. I told Bill to go in and ask if they'd serve us and he told me to go in that I looked worse than he did. Well, we decided not to go in; we'd go find a hamburger joint and eat there. I was following Bill down the street and I got hung on a red light. He kept going and we got separated. We drove all over town and I guess he was driving all over, too, looking for us. Finally we pulled into a burger joint and he happened to pull in there too. Well, ole Bill was mad. He said we were hiding from him. I told him we weren't hiding but he stayed mad anyway.

After we ate, we drove around looking for a place to camp. Finally we found a clear looking spot and camped. The next morning we found we were camped in the garbage dump. So what, we slept good.

Bill had to go find more dry ice to pack around his deer. I

guess we got away from Pecos by mid morning. I think we got on in home that evening.

You know, I've heard that when you get separated like we did, it's better to pull over and stop and wait till the other comes by. However, what if both parties pulled over and waited.

MY SECOND COLORADO HUNTING TRIP IN A TRUCK THAT LIKED ALL THE ROAD

In 1959 Henry Daly, C. N. Marsh and I were going to Drake, Colorado hunting. C. N. knew a guy up there who owned a ranch through which we could gain access to the National Forest. Also, he knew a guy who had some mining claims and some cabins in the forest in which we could camp. This fellow's name was John Phillips.

The day we left home, C. N. needed to go by the cotton gin to see about some weights on cotton. While there, we weighed the truck just for fun. The truck weighed 6800 pounds and you could add 475 more pounds when we three got on board. We were really quite heavy.

The truck was a 1959 GMC three quarter ton with a standard 4 speed transmission. I had a service body on it and it was equipped to use LP gas. The tank size was a 67 gallon one. We had all our personal gear stowed in the compartments and a good bit of stuff in the bed.

The day before we left, I went down to the Firestone Store here in town and had a pair of Firestone Super Ground Grip directional tires installed. Victor Maltoes mounted the tires and aired them up. He was having a terrible time getting those three-piece rims together. I don't know why, I always thought they were easy to get together. As I remember, the only tool he was using was a sledgehammer and he pretty well had the paint knocked off the wheels.

Somewhere around two in the afternoon we pulled out heading north. The first thing I noticed was that the truck began weaving all over the road. We stopped to look at the tires and they seemed to be up all right. Well, after fighting the thing for a while, we stopped again to look at the tires and all seemed ok. Late that evening, we stopped at a service station up in north Texas and I asked the station man, "Reckon why this truck is going all over the road?" He pointed at my rear tires and said "them tires." A little more about the tires later on.

We went out of Texas and through a little piece of Oklahoma and into Colorado. It was getting along in the middle of the night and Henry was driving and after a while the truck started losing power. Henry complained that it was losing power and I told him we were going up hill. He said we were on flat ground. About that time we passed some sort of sign on the right side and I said, "See there, that sign said we were going up a 10% grade." He said, "Sure doesn't seem like it – it looks flat out there to me." The truck was running out of propane but he didn't know that. After while - after we got down to about 20 MPH I told him to switch to gas. Henry said, "Doing better now." Later in the morning, we found a propane place and we filled the truck and went back on LP.

In Denver, we went to a store that C.N. knew about and did some shopping. I remember buying a jacket there and they both got something in the way of coats too.

We drove on to Drake which is west of Loveland and north of Estes Park. We got to the road that went up the mountain to Mark Roberts' ranch and found it locked. C.N. said, "There is a key somewhere around here; let's look for it." C.N. had been there the year before so that's why he said that. We found a key all right and it let us through. We went up the mountain to the ranch house and found no one home. C.N. knew where the cabins were so we headed that way. We met Mark Roberts and some other guy in an old chevy pickup and they both were as drunk as skunks. Thank goodness, Mark knew who C.N. was. Mark said that they had turned their jeep over and wanted us to come help get it back upright. Somehow, John Phillips was there (the guy who owned the cabin that we were going to camp in) too, because he knew where Mark's jeep was when he described the place where it was. I guess we must have met John right there too. Anyway, when we got to the jeep, it was setting up on its side. John Phillips said that he had cut this road up the mountain back when he first had staked some claims up in the forest, but had cut the road after the other road had been put in. When they cut a road, they push up humps of dirt in it so you can't drive over it because you would get on high center. Well, Mark had tried to go up around this hump and the jeep turned up on edge. We got it pushed back on its wheels but it would turn right back up on edge when we turned it loose. Mark got in the jeep and said for us to hold it down and push him off the hump. We did and away he went. He was trying to start it but when he let the clutch out, one wheel in front and one in back would turn one way and the other two wheels turned the other way. Of course, when he held the clutch in, the jeep was freewheeling and the road was steep. John Phillips said, "He's going to kill himself; that road is steep and there are several of those humps in it." Well, C.N. and I took off running down the road but we never saw Mark until we got to the bottom, all the way down to Drake. We figured we'd see where he crashed down that mountain most anyplace. The other guys came down via the good road. Mark wanted to pull it and start it. Every time they tried it, it would break the little chain they had. Finally, they decided to leave it there and go back up to the ranch. Well, the next day after Mark sobered up, he knew what was wrong. When it was turned up, the engine oil had gone past the pistons and locked the engine up. He said that he had turned a truck over one time and it locked up like that and you take the spark plugs out and pump the oil out and then go from there. They went down and did that with the jeep and got it going. You might go to the science of the thing – air will compress but oil will not.

We sat up camp in one of John's cabins. After unloading the pickup we wondered just how much driving around we could do. We let the rear tires down to where they squatted just a little and we found that we could go just about anywhere we wanted. John told us that after it snowed, he'd come up and bring his jeep and stay with us and we'd do some real hunting.

I killed a nice buck. There were lots of deer there on Mark's place but we didn't see any elk. After a few days, it snowed and John came up in his jeep and stayed with us. We asked him how long it would be after it snowed that the elk would come down from the high country. He said "next day." However, it didn't work that way this time. There was a good cover of snow on the ground and we were riding around in John's jeep. All at once, John stopped and said, "There is a bear track." As we were looking at the tracks, we noticed a small spruce sapling that was about 7 feet high and had been ladened with snow and was bent over, making an arch about 3 or 4 feet high. Henry asked John, "How come that bear went under that little arch and didn't knock the snow off of it." Ole John stuttered a little and said, "I guess it wasn't a bear - must have been something else." After looking a little closer, we decided it was a snowshoe rabbit track.

Later on, Henry and C.N. were off walking and hunting and they came up on a cow elk someone had killed and they had field dressed it and propped it open so it would cool out. They thought it had been there two or three days and figured whoever killed it didn't want it or couldn't find it so they cut the two hams off and carved out the backstraps and brought it to camp. They decided not to store the meat at camp in case of company so they took it to John's dynamite house to store it. It was a little ways from the cabin in the side of a steep place – sort of a dugout hole in the ground that had doors on it.

The next day at noon, we cut some steaks off the backstrap and fixed steak and made brindle gravy – boy, you talk about something good! There ain't no better kind of eat'n.

We had just finished eating when a jeep drove up to our camp. These two guys got out and came in. They said they were looking for a jeep of a certain color and license number – they had an emergency message for them. There was one steak left there on the stove and one of the game wardens asked if we were through eating. We said we were so he grabbed a couple slices of bread and put that steak between them and had at it. I could just hear him asking, "Who got the elk?" But he didn't. They did ask if we were hunting and when we said yes, they wanted to see our licenses. There was a tag off mine so they wanted to see my deer. No problem, it's in the building out back. Fine and dandy.

We had been here for about two weeks. A weekend was coming up so I decided to go up to Cheyenne, Wyoming to visit my aunt and uncle. It was only about 65 miles up there. I went and spent one night with them. That next day at noon she had a moose roast and that was some kind of good. There was a pretty good chunk of it left so I asked her if I could take it back to camp with me. She said "Sure you can take it." That night back at camp I told Henry and C.N. that I had some moose roast.

After they ate some of it they both said that wasn't moose, it was beef. I told them I didn't think my aunt would lie to me. At any rate, it was some kind of good stuff.

There were two hunters from Corpus Christi, Texas who came up to Mark Roberts' place to hunt. They got two horses from Mark and one of them killed a bull elk. They came over to ask John Phillips about using his jeep to go after it. There were lots of coyotes in that country and they were worried about them eating their meat. John told them he didn't think they would bother it. He told them the coyotes would eat the guts first and wouldn't bother the carcass because of more human scent on it. I really don't think human scent would matter if they found it. Besides, it was after dark and everybody was tired.

The next morning we all went in John's jeep and loaded the bull in. The driver and the bull were the only ones that rode. The jeep was loaded and there was no room for anything else. They took the bull to Mark's barn and when we all got there, we hung it up and that was the biggest looking thing I'd ever seen. I'm going to say that bull crowded a thousand pounds on foot.

We had planned to pack up and start home that afternoon but those guys said they were through hunting and we could use the horses the rest of the day. We jumped at that chance so C.N. and I rode horses the rest of the day. We covered a lot of country that we hadn't seen when we were hunting on foot. I saw one nice bull but didn't get a chance at him. He was smarter than I was.

We hunted till dark and when we got to Mark's place, Henry was waiting and wanted to pack up and leave. I never dreamed we'd start home after that workout but C.N. said, "You're not waiting on me." So- - - we went to camp and ate something and packed up and left.

With the truck loaded with our gear and a deer on top of that, those tires we had let down really did appear low now. Ok, we'll air them up when we get to Drake. Going down the mountain from Mark's was a slow go – it was slushy and icy and lots of sharp curves and turns. Henry and C.N. were right on their toes telling me just how to drive. Well, when we got to Drake, the one and only service station was closed and air hoses taken in.

We got on blacktop here and within ten seconds, these two back seat drivers were asleep. On better road now and with a little speed the truck was taking all the road weaving around and very uncomfortable to drive. Coming to a curve, I saw a sign pointing to my right and I was thinking the curve was on the other side of it. But no, the curve was on this side of the sign and I had to take it at a greater speed than I would have had it been the other way. Well, when I made the curve a little too fast, the low tires must have laid over and made me feel like I went into a skid. These two backseat drivers woke up and wanted to know what was happening. I told them to go back to sleep, it scared me too. In a little bit we got to Estes Park and there were no open stations and no air. We went on and came to Boulder and believe it or not, we found an air hose with live air. The station was closed but the air was there. I was about 13/11 mad so I put 70 pounds of air pressure in the rear tires. Thought I'd get plenty while I had the chance. I want you to know, that truck straightened up and drove like a GMC is supposed to drive. I really learned something here about the way a vehicle acts. I'm talking about truck tires, not automobile tires. Ever after that when a truck of mine wanted to weave around on the road, I'd check the pressure in the tires.

The rest of our journey home went well. All in all, we had a nice trip even though we brought only one deer home and a little elk meat and I learned something to remember.

CORNBREAD DISAPPOINTMENT

The cornbread in this story comes much later, but is the thing that reminded me of the story.

The story starts out with three of us going to Colorado to hunt deer and elk. Bill Brennan, Henry Daly, and I are the three characters making up the whole thing.

In 1967 I bought a new truck. It was a ¾ ton GMC 4 x 4. I sometimes needed 4 x 4 in my work but also had in mind using it in Colorado. Henry also bought himself a new vehicle that year and it was a 4 x 4 in the Jeep line. It wasn't the little universal C5 jeep but a longer wheel base and more suitable for traveling. He had gotten the full carryall type cab and the half cab. For this trip however, he had the full cab on. I told him we didn't need his jeep because my truck had plenty room for the three of us to ride in and carry all our stuff. Well, a guy with a new toy just had to go in his jeep and alone and Bill and I went in my truck. Henry also had a carrier rack on top so he put on some mesquite wood so he would have something good to burn in our campfire. The aspen and spruce wood up there burns like paper and leaves no coals.

Our first day's journey got us to within 10 miles of Santa Fe, New Mexico. There was a nice gravel pit where we stopped and that is where we pitched our tent and spent the night. At supper I pulled out a jar of hot chili peppers that I had put up at home. I asked the guys if they wanted a chili and they took one each. Bill ate his without a comment but Henry fussed about it being hot and spit and sputtered a little but finally got it all down. We ate one most every meal and Henry once told me that I was going to make a pepper belly out of him yet.

During the night, the wind blew enough to get under the floor of the tent and rattle quite a bit but I think I slept pretty good in spite of it. When the alarm went off next morning, Bill said he had been waiting all night for that alarm to go off. He told us that he wanted us to take him into town to the bus station and he was going back home. He said his heart had bothered him all night. Henry and I talked him into going to see a doctor and see what was going on – see if it was his heart or maybe something else. We found a hospital there in Santa Fe and the doctor on duty said she really didn't feel qualified to take Bill's case so called another doctor. This doctor told Bill that he definitely should not go up in the high country. Furthermore, he ought to stay there in the hospital for observation. Well, Bill sure didn't want to do that but Henry and I talked him into staying.

Henry and I proceeded on toward Colorado arriving in Pagosa Springs mid afternoon. We bought our hunting license and headed northwest towards the high country. We reached the Williams Creek campground area but went on north and west. We were going up a pretty well traveled road (logging road) when night began to fall. We figured we better find a level spot and pitch our tent before dark so we could see what we were doing. The only place we could find was kind of out on a point and vulnerable to the wind and cold as the dickens. We pitched the tent and decided we'd better fix something to eat. We fixed some soup and decided we needed some body in it so decided to put some longhorn cheese in it. It was so cold that it didn't take more'n 2 or 3 minutes to cool off after taking it off the stove and that longhorn cheese became stringy – so bad that we couldn't spoon it and I think we had to use our fingers to get it in our mouths. Well, they made fingers before spoons anyway. We made our beds and went to bed.

Next morning after getting up we began to make our breakfast and discovered all our water wasn't water anymore, it was ice. I mean everything was froze solid. There wasn't any snow on the ground that we could melt for water so we chipped ice out of one of the containers in order to melt for coffee. This kind of camping is not too much fun so we had to keep telling each other how much fun we were having.

With breakfast over, we packed up and went on up the road. We passed a logging camp up the way and then after several more miles up the mountain, we came to a place where a logging camp had been. There was one small cabin setting on this location. I guess it was a bunkhouse – about enough room for two beds. Two windows had been takes out but the door was still on it. We thought that this cabin would be a good place to camp but thought we better ask someone about it first. So, we drove all the way back down to the logging camp that we had passed – some ten miles at least. We saw a pickup coming in behind us so stopped and talked to this guy. We asked about the cabin we had seen and he told us that he couldn't tell us that we could camp there but that the cabin was not going to be moved. OK, we went back up there and set up camp in the cabin. We tacked cardboard over the holes where the windows were taken out and had a nice place to camp. By now it was nightfall again and time to turn in. The next morning we got in Henry's jeep to drive around and right off I saw a nice 4 x 4 buck going up a clearing that had been logged. I had my 6mm Remington along and when Henry stopped, I took a crack at him and had a misfire. It's really a surprise when a cartridge doesn't pop when you pull the trigger. No problem here though, I cranked another one in and got him this time. We dressed him out and hid him in a log pile pretty close to the road.

Most everyday we would drive up the road as far as we could and then a ways down from camp hoping maybe we could bag some game the easy way. We also did a lot of walking. When going out very far on foot I seem to be hoping I wouldn't kill anything because I would have a lot of work getting it back to camp. One day as we were driving up the road, we met 4 or 5 people coming up the road on foot. We stopped to talk to them and they said they were from a camp or lodge a good ways below and had driven to the roadblock and were just walking around to see what they could see. One of the men noticed Henry's glasses case in his shirt pocket which had his name and Crystal City, Texas on it. This guy said, "Crystal City, Texas, I have a brother who lives in Crystal City." His brother was O.L. Tolman. O.L. lived about four miles up highway 83 north of Crystal and a half-mile west. He had a little farm there and had lots of bees around over the country. Everybody around here called him "The Bee Man."

Come that next weekend, a couple guys came to our cabin figuring on camping in our cabin. They were just a little put out when they found a couple Texans camped there. We invited them to have coffee with us before the evening hunt and they accepted. They loosened up a little and they said they weren't prepared to camp in the open. Well, we pitched our tent for them and loaned them some of Bill's gear and then invited them to have supper with us after our hunt. They had hauled a donkey up with them in case they killed something very far off the road. Seemed like a good idea to me. After our evening hunt, Henry and I fixed a whole ham off that buck that I had killed. We had a platter of steak you wouldn't believe. After all that food these guys loosened up and we really enjoyed visiting with them. One of them worked for the logging company that we had asked about the cabin and the other one worked for another company. They were both truck drivers and told a lot of their experiences. One of them said that sometimes the company would harvest a little camp meat out of season and sometimes a game warden would get a little nosy. All you had to do to get that noise stopped was to crowd him just a little with one of them logging trucks and he wouldn't be back very soon.

One day at camp, we had a nice fire going with some of Henry's mesquite wood. All at once, Henry had an idea. "Let's make some cornbread." OK, he went in and mixed up the batter. But first, he told me to put the dutch oven on and get it plenty hot. Told me to put plenty coals on the lid - that it really needed to be hot – had to preheat it real good. OK, I did and here he comes with the batter. When I lifted the lid with a long object he started putting the batter in. It was smoking as soon as it hit the hot oven and then he told me to put the lid on and put plenty coals on it. About the time I got it closed up and more coals on it I asked him how long it needed to bake. He said he'd go look on the box and came back and said it needed about 25 minutes. I said, "Maybe we ought to look at it now." He didn't want me to open it but I did anyway. Well, you guessed it, it was already ashes. It burned that stuff plum up. I'll go along with a hot oven but at the melting stage? I've observed dutch oven baking since then and this guy that did it dug a hole in the ground just a bit larger than the oven and put just a few coals under it and just a few on the lid. His bread came out a beautiful golden brown. Henry and I even cooked some popcorn in a pressure cooker like you would cook beans. We had no idea how long to cook it so we looked at it after 30 minutes at 10 pounds pressure. It was nothing like tender so we cooked it some more. I think we ended up cooking it about 2 hours at 10 pounds (much longer than beans) and it still wasn't tender. You could eat it but that's about it. I guess we were crazy but we were just seeing what it would do. I wouldn't recommend it for company.

The third day we camped here, we went into Pagosa to call down to the hospital where we had left Bill. They informed us that he had checked out that morning and was on his way home. We then called home and I told Ruth to call Myrtle, Bill's daughter-in-law, and tell her what was going on. I was almost sure that he had already called them. As I remember, soon after he arrived home, he got word that a sister of his who lived in Mexico, Missouri was very seriously ill. He jumped in his little VW Bug and headed north. I don't remember if he drove up there or if he went to Waco where his daughter lived and then flew from there. At any rate, he said he got there in time to talk to her before she passed away.

After we had camped at this place a week or more we decided to go down to lower country. Someone had told us that they thought the deer had migrated to lower country and told us of a good area to go to. We decided to make one more drive up and down the road the next day and then pack up and change locations. We were going toward the roadblock when I saw a deer. It was on Henry's side and I told him to shoot it. He didn't see it and thought I was pulling his leg. Well, I stepped out of the jeep and took a rest across the hood and touched it off. I shot the deer in such a place that it dropped in its tracks. Henry still didn't see the deer and thought I was trying to fool him. We drove on down to where the road was blocked (I don't remember how the road was blocked – if it was fallen trees or a caved out place or what.) turned around and headed back. When we got up to where I had shot the deer I told Henry to drive out there to get my deer. He wouldn't do it because he still thought I was pulling one on him. I did get him, however, to walk out there with me and he finally saw the deer. We dressed it out and loaded it in the jeep and went back to camp. We packed up our stuff and were going to head for lower country.

We were in the San Juan National Forest and would still be in it when we went to lower country. It really wasn't too many miles the way the crow flies, but by road it was a half-day drive. We drove back to Pagosa Springs and then west on highway 160 taking us to Bayfield where we turned north following the Los Pinos River. We traveled nearly to Vallecito Reservoir and then east on a road taking us to the Graham Creek area. We could see the Vallecito Reservoir when we were up in the higher country but it was a lot of miles down below us. Here we were in Aspen country with some Spruce here and there. We made camp and got our freshly killed deer hung up and by the next morning it was plenty cold – maybe not frozen but cold enough. In driving around the next day, we came to a tall watchtower. The attendant hollered down to us to come on up and visit. We went up and really enjoyed the visit. She explained to us just what her duties were and about the equipment we saw there. I guess her main duty was to watch for fires and report the exact location if any occurred. She said there had been lots of hunters camped in the area earlier. We asked about their campfires. She said there is lots of difference between a campfire and a forest fire. She said a campfire never gets any bigger but a forest fire flares up into the trees and can be spotted immediately.

We drove all the roads we could find in that area and as I remember we didn't see any game. There was one little road we saw that looked pretty tuff to get on. It was a steep hill right off the main road and loose dirt too and, I guess, presented a challenge. I told Henry to give it a try. We had nothing to lose; we had a winch on front if we needed it. He headed his jeep up the steep place and made it OK. Oh, he spun around a little but made it all right. We didn't know it right then but that was the easy part. After following this road with all its turns and steep places and sometimes a lot of side fall we came to a place that was kinda hairy. The road was leaning right smart and there was a washed out gully in front of us. Vehicles had been going across it but Henry was scared to try it. He couldn't back down the road because it was very crooked and steep in places and a bad side fall in places. Well, finally he decided to try it. First though, we payed out some cable off his winch and tied it to a tree on the up side and then he wished for a winch on the rear too. I told him that I'd get out in front, and for him to watch me and I'd watch his wheels and motion to him just how to steer and for him to come on toward me and whatever he did – just keep moving slowly and by all means don't stop. Well, he'd move a little and stop and invariably the jeep would slide sideways a little. Finally he made it over that bad place but he was upset by this time. He blamed me for taking him up that road with his new jeep and that he had all that money tied up in it. I told him that I was sorry but I thought we both wanted to go up that road. It wasn't far up the road when we broke out into some real pretty open park type country. I wanted to go on and look around more but he wasn't a bit interested in looking around. He just wanted to get out of there and back to the main road. Of course that meant we had that bad place to cross again and go through all the moaning and groaning and me getting blamed for wanting to come up that road. I figured if we had gone on ahead and looked around that open country for an hour or two, he would have cooled off a little before we had to cross it again. Who knows, we might have found a better road back down the mountain.

We camped in this area 2 or maybe 3 nights and saw no game at all. We decided we had had enough hunting so we packed up and headed for Texas. When we got down to Sanderson, Texas, Henry decided to go west to Presidio and visit friends and kinfolk – this is where he was raised. I headed my GMC toward Crystal City.

This ended another Colorado hunt that you might say was eventful but not over productive. Two deer in all and a lot of fun. Well, when we look back on it now, we can laugh about it.

GOING DEEP FOR COOL WATER

Back in the mid 60's I bought a boat and motor from Bill Brennan. It was a 14-foot aluminum one and kinda narrow. Best one I'd ever had though. The motor was a small 2 1/2-horse power Johnson. Ideal for running lines.

My son Ed was about 12 or 13 years old and his friend Dwight Cook was a few weeks older. The boys wanted to come down the river and I had promised them that we would. The river had been on a rise and was running very strong. We'd go check the water level at the crossing where we put in once in a while. At that time the Batesville road went over this low water crossing - a concrete slab with 6 or 8 big horns under it. The water would still be up on the slab and I 'd tell them that it's still too much water. I'm sure they didn't understand. The looks of it there didn't seem like too much water to them. Finally I told them when the water stopped running over the cement, we'd do it.

In a few days we decided to do it. We got our gear together - motor and gas, food and cookware, and tent and bedding and fishing gear. The day finally arrived and away we went. Ed was handling the motor and I was in the bow so I could push away from things. We came to a place that narrowed and got swift and there was a drift hung on a grapevine and we had to make a 90-degree to the right. I got the boat turned all right but Ed some how lost control. He saw that he was going to hit the drift so he put his legs up to keep from hitting the drift and when he hit it, it knocked him right out of the boat. The boat and motor went under the drift a little and thank goodness, the brush knocked the throttle down to stop. The throttle was on the motor right in front of the little gas tank. Ed came right up and grabbed the side of the boat and I somehow got the boat out of the drift. I think it scared Dwight more than it did Ed. It all happened so fast we really didn't have time to think. I tell you what, you've heard of split second decisions. Dwight was hollering to Ed, "You alright - you alright?" I really believe after that, the boys realized how danger appears and quick most of the time.

We camped at the Evans Lake a couple nights. We set lines

but don't remember much about the fish except we did catch one big ole needle nose gar. I've got a picture of it somewhere.

In those days, we never thought of carrying drinking water from home. We always drank river water. We had some of those army canteens with canvas covers and if you'd keep the cover wet and in the wind, it would keep the water nice and cool. And too, the water seemed to be cooler down deep so we'd dive down and fill our canteens.

RODS AND REELS DO SINK

Long years ago, my Dad, Nick Roberts and Uncle Rueben Donnell went fishing up on the river. They put in at the Averhauff Landing. The water was way down in the channel and all the log piles were visible in the bottom of the river. They went down stream and fished around a lot of those logs. During the course of the day, Nick Roberts lost a rod and reel in the river. I don't know if a fish jerked it out of his hand or if he laid it down and a fish pulled it in or if he just plain dropped it. Any way, they couldn't retrieve it. They worked at it but to no avail.

In a few days, I was going up there to fish and Dad told me which log pile he had lost it at and about how deep the water was. I took a piece of barbed wire and made a loop about four feet long kinda in an oval shape. I found the log pile he was talking about and got in the position he told me their boat was in and which side of the boat Nick was sitting on. I reached down with the loop and I want you to know, I caught that rod the very first drag. I brought it back to Nick and he was very happy about getting it back.

Another little story along this same line - my Uncle Lester from Cheyenne was visiting and he had bought himself one of those little bitty rod and reel outfits that was about 18 inches long. He was really anxious to go up on the river and try it. You know, they advertised those things telling you that you can carry them in your pocket and you're always ready to catch a fish anywhere anytime. Well, he, my Dad and Jim went up on the river. Uncle Lester could hardly wait to try out his beauty. The first thing he found out was that he couldn't cast more'n about ten feet with it. Jim started teasing him about it - telling him that he was going to throw it in the river if he didn't watch out. He reared back and was going to show Jim he could get out there better than he'd been doing and sure enough, he threw it right into the water.

Before he threw it away, he had asked Jim about trading it in on a better outfit. It was brand new and he thought maybe Jim would allow him nearly as much as he had paid for it. Well, any way it was too late now. The last cast had put the finish to it.

BOBCATS IN CAMP

One time J.W. Wilkins was down from North Platte, Nebraska, visiting his family and us. He and I and my Dad went up on the river to spend the night. We put our boat in there at the Averhauff Landing and went down stream a mile or two and up a creek a little ways to camp.

We set our trotlines out and baited them just before dark and then around 11 PM we ran them. We got a few catfish and then parked the boat there by our camp. We went ahead and cleaned the fish and put them on ice. We went up to camp to go to bed. Our bed was nothing more than a wagon sheet laid on the ground (a piece of canvas) to lay on and pull up over us if the mosquitoes were to come and be too friendly. If you had to cover up with that canvas on a summer night, you really sweat it out. However, that was better than mosquitoes.

Sometime after midnight, my Dad woke me up and asked me what that noise was. Henry Voltz's place was across the river and he had hogs that were bumping the automatic feeders once in a while that I could hear. Dad said it wasn't that, it's something else. I went back to sleep and pretty soon a noise woke me up and it sounded like some kind of animals fighting. I told Dad it most likely was some raccoons fighting over the fish heads that we had thrown up on the bank when we cleaned those fish earlier. Well, the growling continued and seemed to be a little closer all the time. I grabbed my flashlight and shined in the direction of the growling. It was not raccoons fighting at all. It was two bobcats and they weren't more than ten yards from us.

This was the first time in my life that I did not take some sort of firearm with me when I went camping. I could have gotten at least one of them and maybe both. Trying to sleep with that going on and close like it was, wasn't easy. In a little bit one of them let out a blood curdling scream and J. W. woke up and sat straight up and wanted to know what was going on.

You know, those cats stayed right there until daybreak. After the break of light, they meandered out into the brush carrying on something awful. Only thing I could figure, it must have been mating season and they didn't need us there at all. I had never had anything like that happen before or since. But you know, there is always a first for everything.

LITTLE HISSING SNAKE

In past years I've seen little snakes out in the yard. They are shiny brown little things. When you catch one they are hard to hold, they are so slippery they can work their way right out of your hand. I think these are the ones that have the full length green and yellow strips and maybe a little red on them too. I think we call them garter or grass snakes. I caught one once and brought it in the house and put it in the sink. He couldn't crawl out so I left him in there. After while Ruth came home and I heard her holler. She came out to where I was and told me to get that thing out of the house. She said that thing was almost standing on his tale hissing and taking on something awful. I guess he'd been in there long enough.

CATCHING PREDATORS

Back in 1930 when we moved to the farm we had all the predators that you could find listed in any book that were adapted to this part of the country and maybe a few more. The ones that bothered us most were bobcats, coyotes, skunks, hawks, and owls. We had chickens that ran loose and we were lucky if we got more of them than the predators did.

I remember Dad putting chickens in a good strong cage and placing it out away from the house and setting steel traps around it. He caught a lot of bobcats and hawks by doing this. The coyote was a much smarter critter and he didn't get many of them this way. The rifle was a much better way if you had time to sit and wait. The raccoons didn't seem to bother chickens much, but they sure played the dickens with corn and other grain crops. The owls (Great Horned Owl) would get in the chicken's roosting house and get a chicken and take it's head off and suck the blood out. We had hogs and a lot of times a hog would catch and eat a chicken when messing around in their pens.

About the easiest way to catch a bobcat, wild housecats, or raccoon is to tie a bait (a bird of some kind) with a good strong wire about four feet off the ground. They'll go to jumping for it and get in the trap that you set under it. You don't even need to hide the trap. There is no way you can catch a coyote like this. For coyotes, you have to kill all human scent by boiling the steel traps and putting clean gloves on and bury the trap. It is very important to leave no human scent. One of the best baits for a coyote is cat urine, either bobcat or housecat.

My Granddad had chickens running loose. The hens would hide their nests and somehow raised their young. He also had a flock of guineas. I don't think the guineas were quite as vulnerable as the chickens. They had a little more instinctive traits about them and could take care of themselves a little better than chickens.

Among the predators, I will name a few more besides the ones I've already mentioned. Opossums, ringtailed cats, badgers, fox, rats and all sorts of snakes and more.

FLOATING RATTLESNAKE

I had bought a boat from Cecil Hancock. It was a 15-foot fiberglass boat with a 45-horse motor on it. Pretty good outfit when you could get it to run, but doing that is another story in itself. Maybe later.

Ruth and I went down to Falcon Lake near Zapata. A young couple who worked at the Carrizo Springs hospital where Ruth worked came down to spend a night with us and do a little fishing.

At Zapata we took the road that went to Old Zapata and that's where we put the boat in the water and we camped nearby.

Mainly, we fished for white bass. The most productive way to do that is watch for the seagulls. When you see a bunch of gulls diving into the water that means they are diving for the bait fish that the bass are feeding on and they are pushed to the surface and the gulls are feeding on them. If you get there quick enough, you can catch a fish every cast. Really doesn't matter what kind of bait you use - they'll take it.

This couple went home in the afternoon and Ruth and I stayed another night. The next morning, we decided to go boat riding down the lake. We had gone a couple miles or so when we saw something floating in the water. At first, I thought it looked like a bicycle tire floating. When we got to it, it wasn't a tire at all - it was a rattlesnake! The snake was in a circle with his head laying on his body. He was just floating - taking it easy. We went close to him and I started poking at him and he came alive. He coiled up just the same as if he was on land. He would strike at the object I was teasing him with. I wished for my camera - why I didn't bring it along in the first place I can't say. Anyway, we decided to go back after it. I took note of the marker we were close to and took off back to camp to get the camera. I suppose we were gone twenty or thirty minutes. When we got back to the area where we'd seen the snake I couldn't find it. I had noticed a Mexican fisherman running his nets three or four hundred yards from us before we went for the camera. After I couldn't find the snake I looked for the fisherman. I saw him over there a ways hitting at something.

We went over to him and discovered he was killing our snake. He said that he watched us circling around something and after we left, he went to see what it was. He held the snake up for me to take pictures. I asked him if they had snakes in Mexico. He said the only ones they had were the ones like this one that floated over from Texas. If you believe that, stand on your head.

The night before, after we had gone to bed, about 11 PM we heard voices. I got up and looked out and I saw what I thought was a boat out in the water about where the Old Zapata highway went into the lake. I thought it was some people fishing. The light never moved. In a little while, a truck came down the road and turned around and backed up to the edge of the water. I saw some guys walk to the rear of the truck and then start wading out toward the light in the lake. I guess, what I thought was a boat was a car that had driven right on down the road right into the water. It was out in there about fifty or so yards and these guys were pulling a cable from this winch truck out to the submerged car and pulled it out with the winch.

The highway department had placed two sets of bars in the road a little ways before getting to the water. Whoever was in the car must have been stoned because running over those bars at any speed at all would rattle ones brain loose.

A DOG THAT LOVED THE RIVER TRIP

One time on a river trip I brought my nephew Dwight, my son-in-law, Ron Small, and my dog named Spook. Spook was a Beagle type dog with a little part of some kind of larger dog. We had some rain as we were going down river and I'd put a plastic tarp over Spook and he seemed to know why I covered him.

One of the things I remember about this trip was about some of the cooking. When I fry potatoes I'd sooner have them a little underdone rather than overdone. Well, Ron didn't like them the way I did them so he said he'd do them the next time. The next time we were going to have potatoes he was going to do them. I watched him so I'd know next time just how to do them. He constantly turned them as they were cooking and they got soggy as well as overdone. When we were eating them, my nephew told me that he liked mine better than Ron's. I told him I liked mine better too. Maybe the dog liked them all right. He'd eat anything you gave him off the table.

On another river trip, Bruce Ivey and I and the dog were doing this one together. We were at the lower end of the Evans Lake catching minnows. The water was running strong - the long rapid there was about 18 inches deep and 20 feet wide and running swift. Well, ole Spook decided he needed on the other side. He barreled in to swim across and the swift water took him 30 or 40 yards down stream before he reached the other side. It seemed that he had a funny expression on his face. He got back all right - I don't remember watching him come back.

On another occasion Ruth and I took Spook in the big boat. We put in at the Averhauff Landing and went up stream several miles. We set out three trotlines and then we camped. We found a little flat spot up on the bank and set up our kitchen on it. We slept in the boat. Our boat was brand new and I had gone up to San Antonio that morning to buy the rear curtain and side windows. I had the top already. The boat already had all the snaps that were needed so these pieces zipped in and snapped in real nice. Sure enough it rained on us so we were glad that we had purchased the pieces.

We were returning from baiting our trotlines that first evening and as we approached camp, we heard and saw turkeys flying to roost right over our kitchen. Well, next morning at first light, they started flying off their roost. Ole Spook didn't know what was happening. In the night, we heard Spook growl with a low tone and then we thought we heard something make a noise in the kitchen. I opened the front of the boat and told Spook to go check it out. His sleeping spot was up on the motorwell cover. In a flash he went out the front of the boat and went up the bank snuffing and growling; turned around and came back in and up on his bed he went.

NOT WORTH THE TROUBLE, OR WAS IT?

On an occasion my brother Jim, his son Jimmy, and I came down the river. We put the boat in at the old La Pryor-Batesville crossing and headed down river from there. There are lots of pretty little holes of water along the way and we cast into most of them. We got a fish here and there and when we got to the Kingfisher Hole, you can expect to get several nice ones. On down another mile or so we came to the Evans Lake. It is a beautiful piece of water with willows lining both banks and several places you will see lily pads. Bait fish hang around and hide in the clumps of lily pads and the game fish are around there waiting to catch a meal. Once in a while a bass will get excited and grab your bait when you cast it near the lily pads.

We had a tent to put up so decided to do that as it was getting late - we needed to eat too. I mentioned that I had brought some setlines and we had already scooped up some minnows to bait them with - shall we set them out? Jim said "Nah, we wouldn't catch anything anyway." Jimmy said, "Yeah, Daddy and Uncle Dale, lets do, it won't take long." OK, we tied them out and baited them and went back to camp. We were tired so didn't bother to run them in the night. Next morning we went to run them and take them up. Well, we had a nice stripper, a real nice crappie, and a couple nice channels (catfish) and a 20 pound flathead. The flathead cat is the best catfish they make. Jimmy asked his Dad if it was worth it and Jim said, "Sure was."

My setlines were made of green nylon string and when tied to the green willow limbs, you can't find them when you come back. So, I took clothespins and tied white flags to them and it's very easy to pin a flag to the limb where you put the line.

After cleaning our catch and putting them on ice, we went casting. Down on the lower end of the lake there are lots of lily pads and usually produce some nice bass. Jimmy had borrowed a crippled shad lure from me and he got a heck of a good bass on it. I told him that I got half the credit on getting that big bass because it was my bait. He said he didn't care what he had to do, he had all the fun catching and landing it. I said I guessed there wasn't anyway I could take half the fun.

OVERCAST SKIES TURNED INTO A VICIOUS STORM

Bruce Ivey and I were going to make a one-day run down the river. We got Lloyd Williamson to take us up to where we launch the boat between La Pryor and Batesville. Just as soon as we got all our gear out of the truck into the boat, Lloyd took off for home.

The weather had been overcast for a week or more and really nice for this kind of activity. Well, I believe before we fired up the motor on the boat, we heard thunder. Now, with Lloyd gone there wasn't but one way home and that was down the river. We got about a mile down and a thunderstorm found us. There was a nice hole of water where we were and a steep bank to our right so we set the storm out. The wind blew and it rained and hailed some. To say the least, we were cold and couldn't do anything about it. The storm passed over so we headed out again. I guess we got 3 or 4 hundred yards further down and it came again. I don't know if it was another storm or that one had backed up on us or what. The way the river winds around, you can't tell sometimes which direction you are pointing. Anyhow, it came a good one - I mean it rained, blew, hailed, the lightning was fierce and of course the thunder was very steady. We had pulled the boat up on a gravel bar. In a little bit, I noticed it was leaving. I jumped in the water to grab it and the water felt so warm, I laid down in the water. I hollered to Bruce to come in too; it's a lot warmer than standing out in the rain and wind. He had on a short sleeve shirt and thin too. He was shaking so bad that I wondered what might happen to him. The storm finally passed on and we headed on down the river. The rain had washed so much trash off the banks into the water that we couldn't cast so we went a little faster to see if we could get ahead of the trash. We stopped to catch some minnows before getting into the Upper Nueces Impoundment thinking maybe we could fish a little around some brush piles in the deeper water. It worked out pretty good; we got a nice stringer of bass to take home. We made it to the Landing at the appointed time and loaded up and headed for home.

Some thirty or more years ago our pastor of our church suggested that the deacons treat their wives to a fish fry. To give you an idea of the period of time it was; Mr. H. R. McNeil, my Dad, Ed Walker, and several of the older gents were still active at the time. This will give you older ones who knew those guys an idea of how long ago it was.

I had become pretty well acquainted with Bruce Ivey so I invited him to come down the river with me and we'd do our best to get enough fish for the big fish fry. Bruce told me that he had been down the river back in 1936. He and his brother, Maury, and Billy Brennan came through there but didn't remember much about it. He didn't say anything about fishing.

We got all our gear together and headed for the river. We put in between La Pryor and Batesville - the old crossing.

We set up camp at the Evans Lake and set out three trotlines and baited the hooks with frogs that we caught the night before. About midnight, we ran the lines. Off of one line, we took ten catfish. I'm sure we must have taken some off the others too. The next morning we got a few more. We went back to camp and set in the boat and filleted fish until noon. I don't remember how many we got the second night but I'm sure we got some. The pastor said that he would pray that we catch enough fish for the "fry" and later he said that he did. Bruce wasn't a deacon but he was invited because he sure participated in the work part.

On another occasion Bruce and I came down the river and camped close to the upper end of the Evans Lake. There had been a pump location dozed out near the water and there was a nice flat spot there to put up our tent. After we pitched our tent and camp set up, we decided to walk up the road that followed a cut that had been dozed out for the water pipe to lay in. Bruce went a few minutes before I went. Walking up the cut, there was a rod and reel with its line tangled up in the brush hanging right there in plain sight. Bruce wanted to know where I found that. I told him and he said that he had walked up that cut before I did and he didn't see it. If one held his head up at all, he'd see it.

There are some real good looking places or holes of water before getting to the Evans Lake that I have always wanted to fish but never had. I told Bruce we were going back up there and set some lines. We did it and it was hard because the current was swift and we had to get out of the boat and pull it up the current. Ole Bruce wanted to give it up but I didn't. We set three trotlines up there and the sad part about it was, I don't remember catching a single fish. To say the least, we moved those lines. A funny thing happened when we set those lines; we had set one pretty close to camp and then went up stream to set the others and baited them on the way back. On the one next to camp, we had a fish on one of the hooks. There must have been a small piece of dried stuff on the hook or the fish wasn't looking where he was going. We set the lines from above down in the main lake.

The next morning, I woke up an hour or more before daylight. I thought my eyes were playing tricks on me. There was a steady flicker of lightening. I mean steady - no breaks in it at all. I woke Bruce up and told him there was a cloud some where that sure had lots of lightening in it so maybe we better get up and get our breakfast and pack camp up and go get our lines up. By this time we could hear thunder and plenty of it. We took the one up that was close to camp and then went down lake to get the others. Boy, I tell you by the time we got about half of the lines down lake taken up the storm was just about upon us. A lightening bolt hit just about where camp was and then it came right on down on us. Lightening was striking all around us. The banks and tall trees were so much higher than we were I kept telling myself we were safe down on the water. Finally it passed over and we finished getting our lines up and went back up to camp and packed up the boat and headed down river toward home.

On another occasion several years earlier, my brother Jim, James Powell, Ruth's youngest brother, and I made a river trip. We got to the Evans Lake and were in a hurry to get camp set up for there was a cloud coming up. We didn't get the tent up before it wet us good. I don't remember anything about the fishing. There were several storms around and we may not have fished.

The plan was, the next day Dr. Spencer was coming up from below to meet us as we came down. We were going to fish together and camp together that night. With all the storms in the area, I didn't think he'd come.

Along in mid to late afternoon, there he was. He told us there had been a pretty bad storm near town the evening before - had taken some of the roof off Kermitt Marshall's shop north of town. We asked him if he didn't think maybe we ought to go on home because of all the storms around. He said, "There is nobody looking for me at home tonight." OK, we stayed and set out a few lines. I don't think we caught any fish and I don't remember if it rained on us. Yeah, come to think of it, it did rain too. Seems like I've heard too that fish don't bite in stormy weather - they hide out so they don't get wet. Kinda like a turtle that climbs up on a log to sun himself. If it starts to rain, he slides into the water to keep from getting wet. We had fun though - I remember telling each other how much fun we're having. Everyone agreed to that.

TIN CANS DO CUT

Ruth and I along with Ed and Katy were coming down the river just for a one-day trip. We were casting into most of the good look'n places trying for bass. We stopped at this one place to try for minnows with the seine and while stopped, we decided to eat lunch. The time was something after 11 AM. Ed was opening a can of pork'n beans and somehow, he cut one of his hands real bad. He bled like a stuck hog. We worried about it because we had most of the trip ahead of us yet.

We arrived at our favorite fishing place on Evans Lake and caught a nice bunch of crappie and then eased on down river reaching the Averhauff Landing at the appointed time.

Bill Carruthers wanted to come through the river so I planned a trip with him. The water was low and we had a lot of getting out to do and pulling the boat through the shallow rapids. This sort of thing runs into work when you have to get out at every one of them. It takes lots of the fun out of the trip.

We camped at the Evans Lake a couple nights and did our fishing. Ole Bill was complaining about the work and knew there was lots more of it to do. He said that he was just going to walk out of there. I asked him if he would leave me all by myself and all that work getting the boat on down the river. He said he sure would. If you happen to know Bill, you know he makes lots of noise about things.

Third day as we were pulling on through and I mean "pulling" I found a gas lantern in one of the rapids. The glass was knocked out of it. It had been in there a year or more because it had a good coating of moss on it. The gas tank seemed to be full - I figured water. I opened it and it was gas and it smelled just as fresh as if you'd just poured it full. I threw the thing up on the bank but kept the lid - it's still in my tackle box.

KEEP YOUR EYES OPEN AND YOU MAY FIND SOMETHING

Ruth and I were making the river trip. We had camped at Evans Lake and had done our fishing and were coming on through. About 30 minutes below the lake if the water is running nice, there is a real nice hole. We always like to cast coming through this one and usually pick up a nice bass or two. At the lower end of this hole, there is narrow and shallow stretch of river about a hundred yards long or maybe a little more. There is a flat bench on the left the length of it and there are (were) a lot of willow trees along it. Well, someone had dozed all those trees into the river. I can just see them having fun knowing how much grief they were giving people like us. A lot of times we would bring a chainsaw with us if there had been a rise and thinking there might be new tree falls in the water. This time, I had only a hatchet. We had to get through there or go up around. It really wasn't nearly as bad as it first appeared. We were walking the boat through and I had to cut a limb here and there but not all that much. Anyway, while walking the boat, I looked down and found a rod and reel. It had been in there a while; there was moss all over it and the rod was broken off in front of the handle. Surprisingly it cleaned up real good. It was a Garcia 5000 bait casting reel. Pretty good find.

I was telling Royce Cook about finding a reel up there and he said he knew who lost it. He said Dr. Stauber had lost a Garcia reel in the river up there a couple years before. Who knows, I suppose there have been more than that one lost in there.

TO GO HOME YOU KEEP ON GOING AHEAD

On one river trip our pastor, Ronny Waycaster, my grandson, Jarrod, and I were fishing our way down the river. We were catching fish right along but I couldn't get Jarrod interested in trying to fish. I had rigged up a spinning casting outfit for him but he wouldn't try.

'Long about 11 AM Jarrod was wanting to go home. I told him we were on the way home but he thought we had to turn around and go back the way we came to go home. After a little while he settled down. In a little while right out of the bright blue sky, he said, "You catch more fish than my Dad does but the ones he catches are bigger." I told him that was fine and that I was glad. It wasn't long after this conversation that he picked up a knife and started cleaning our fish. He was doing a pretty good job so Ronny and I bragged on him. To my surprise, he kept on doing it and did a pretty good job of filleting. I guess he must have gotten something out of it because the next time he was down here he suggested that we come down the river. He even said that he would do all the pulling the boat over the rapids. Well, he came and we did the river trip and he did real good. We even camped two nights on the Evans Lake this time.

Back in high school days three of us made a river trip. This trip was powered by paddles made out of 1 x 6 and lots of elbow grease. The other two were Maurice Oden, whom we called Colorado because he was red headed, and the other was Billy McFall, a friend visiting from Beeville, Texas. Billy had lived here some years before.

We camped two nights on Evans Lake and we put trotlines out. We caught one 18-pound flathead catfish and several others. We could keep only what we could eat because we had no ice to store them in. Sometimes we would try taking a couple home but we had to keep them alive. One day ole Colorado cooked some red beans and he put some green chilies in them. I didn't eat hot stuff in those days nor did Billy. Well, we're setting there eating dinner that day and I guess Billy got one of those hot chilies in his mouth. Boy, he hollered and threw his plate and headed for the river. I told Colorado, "Watch him hit the water with his hat on." Sure enough he did and we were laughing at him when he came up. He asked us "Why didn't we tell him he had his hat on." His mouth was burning so much I don't suppose he would have heard us if we had told him. A big ole straw hat on your head might cause one to jam his neck a little diving in like that. I don't know, I never have done it.

TOO MANY GOOD PLUMS ARE NOT GOOD

Some years ago we had a pastor by the name of Ronny Waycaster. He was a pretty good fisherman and he learned to enjoy hunting while he was here. He and I and my grandson, Matthew, came down the river. We'd go up near La Pryor to put the boat in the river. Coming down the river, we'd fish and camp a couple nights and then we would come out at the Averhauff Landing. Most always, we camped the two nights at the Evans Lake. We set out lines for catfish and there were lots of good places for casting. Crappie were plentiful, too, if you could find an underwater brush pile. One day after we had eaten lunch, I wanted to take a nap so bad I couldn't keep my eyes open. I got out of the boat and went up on the bank and found a clean spot on the ground and laid down and took my nap for about a half-hour. I went back to the boat and Ronny said the gasoline sure was leaking out of the motor. I said, "Man alive, why didn't you stop it?" Said he didn't know how. All you had to do was unplug the gas line from the tank or the motor. Well, he didn't know that. I was concerned about the gas because the trip through there and fooling around there on the lake a couple days would run us pretty short on gas. Well, as it was, we made it through there but I don't think we could have gone a mile farther.

While there at the lake, Matthew got into the groceries and ate a bunch of big purple ripe plums. He said he ate thirteen of them. I didn't know about this until he complained of a bellyache. I think it scared him more than anything. He got OK after running to the woods about three times.

SAYING NO, EVEN BEFORE YOU KNOW WHAT IT IS

Ronny Waycaster, one of our pastors, was helping me work cattle one day. I had several bull calves to cut and do all the other things to. I always saved the "mountain oysters" for further use. We had put a couple mountain oysters on the branding iron heater and let them break open and dry out some and then ate them. I had even taken salt and pepper with me that day. Well, Ronny nibbled around on one and finally said he liked it all right.

I told Ronny that I was going to fix them for supper that night and for them to come over and help eat them. He said he would but he didn't think Kathy would eat any.

I had prepared them by hulling them out and slicing them crossways then rolling them in cornmeal and putting salt, pepper and garlic on them. Now, you talk about something good - they were.

When they came, Kathy wouldn't come close to the kitchen. Finally I got her to smell one and she said she thought that it smelled good but she didn't know about eating it. Finally, I got her to taste one. She said, "Man, that's good." If any of you remember Kathy Waycaster, you will remember when she found something she liked, she wouldn't leave it alone until it was all gone. I opened a jar of smoked salmon one time that I had smoked in Alaska and had processed - she ate the whole thing.

They were the same way about venison when they first came here. They didn't want any part of it. Someone had given them a piece of venison one time and it made them sick. Well, kinda like the mountain oysters, after they tasted some of ours, it changed their whole story about venison.

One time Kathy's Mom and Dad were visiting them and we had them over to eat. Kathy told me that my venison was good and she liked it but she was afraid her Dad wouldn't eat any - he most likely wouldn't even taste it. OK, I went to town and bought some fried chicken just for him. When we sat down to eat, he said that venison sure did smell good - believed he'd taste it. Well, guess who got to eat the chicken? We did - we had it for the next meal. I guess after that, he was here at least a couple times and he'd send word, "Don't even think about having anything other than venison." We've even taken venison up there where they live in Jackson, Tennessee, when we'd stop to visit them on our way to Clarksville, Tennessee.

They said someone had given them some once and it was bad stuff. It most likely was off a deer that had been gut shot, and wasn't trimmed properly and/or the person who cleaned the deer might have gotten the musky scent from the glands on the hind legs on their hands and all around on the meat. It could have been meat off of an old strong deer that was in the rut at the time he was harvested. Any number of things can mess up venison. Any other kind of meat wouldn't be good either if it got treated like that.

Another reason venison is bad stuff is because hunters go out and harvest a deer; shoot it through the body or shoulders or hams and then they don't bother to skin it and cut all that blood-shot stuff out of there and clean it up right away. A lot of times they hang them up and the weather is warm. All that adds up to be bad stuff. Treating game like this would break anyone from eating it. The first thing I do when I harvest a deer is to cut the scent glands off the rear legs, being careful not to get it on my hands. When I get home, I skin it out and split it down the middle and hang it in the cooler. If it's shot through the body, I cut all the bloody stuff away making excellent dog food out of it. There is nothing a dog or cat likes better than this kind of stuff. I've heard people say that they put a shot-up shoulder in the garbage - they didn't feed their dog that kind of stuff.

FISH BEGIN BITING AT 12 NOON

By the title of this story one might think we had the fish on a computerized schedule. Well, not really, but it did really happen - the 12 noon part, I mean.

My son, Ed, and I came through the river to do a little fishing and have a little relaxation. I'm not saying we were having a rest from work because I think if there was a way to count or to measure the output of the human body, we most likely would find out there is a good bit more energy spent doing play stuff than when we work. Make any sense to you?

Getting on with my story - we cast a little here and there on the way down, if and when we get a break from fighting brush and pulling over the rapids. There is a real nice hole of water about half way to the Evans Lake and we have heard it called Kingfisher Hole. I guess it's a quarter-mile long. We go through it slow and do a lot of casting and most always catch several nice bass. Well, this time we didn't get a single one. We decided to motor back to the upper end of it and come through again. When we got up to the end, we decided to eat our lunch. There was a log sticking up out of the water and a good shade there so we tied up and had our lunch. It was after 11:20 when we tied up. Right at noon, we untied the boat and started drifting with the current and casting to both sides of the river. I want you to know, we started catching bass. We caught fish all afternoon all the way to the Evans Lake and even after dark, the bass were hitting. We had thrown back lots of bass but had our share of keepers to bring home. No telling how much work we could have gotten done at home if we had spent that much energy in that same length of time.

WAITING IT OUT PAID OFF

One day my son-in-law, Ron, my grandson, Matthew, and I went out to the farm to hunt deer. Ron took the high stand on the west side and Matthew and I sat in the stand on the tank dump at the northwest corner of the farm. Pretty soon a deer came in the field about sixty yards from us. It was a good size deer and after looking it over, I could see two short spikes. I told Matthew to go ahead and try for him. He shot and the deer went down. Matthew wanted to go right over to him but I wouldn't let him. The deer would move its head ever little bit and Matthew really wanted to go shoot it again. I didn't let him. I said, "Maybe another one will come in, so be quiet." He told me the next one would be mine. It was getting late and I was taking one more look with my binoculars and sure enough, there was one standing and pretty close to Matt's deer. I asked him, "The next one mine?" He said yes. Well, I dropped him and just in a matter of seconds, Ron shot. I told Matthew Ron shot in our direction. He wanted to know how I knew that. I explained that a gun sounds different when it is pointing toward you and in this case, I heard the bullet hit the deer first and then the rifle report.

Matthew and I walked up the hill to get the jeep and came back to our deer. His deer was still alive. He had hit him in the neck but just close enough to the bone to paralyze him. The reason for the short spikes was that both his antlers had been shot off. The deer was big enough to have been at least a six pointer or maybe an eight pointer. Mine was an eight pointer. We loaded both deer on the jeep and went down to Ron. He had shot his buck about one third of the way up toward us which proved to Matthew what I had told him about the direction. Ron's deer was also an eight pointer. I might add, Ron and I shot ours just about two seconds before the thirty-minute after sundown shooting time had expired.

SKINNING CATFISH THE WRONG WAY

One time Gary Kinnard, Bill Brennan and I went up on Amistad Lake. We had gone about thirty miles up from Diablo East boat ramp. We set out a couple trotlines and sat out two wind and rain storms with plenty lightning and thunder. Thunderstorms are quite common on that lake. They come anytime and quick.

Next morning we had taken several catfish off the lines and had gone back to camp to fix some breakfast and clean our fish. Bill said he would start cleaning fish while Gary and I put the breakfast together. In a little while, Gary told me that Bill was trying to skin those fish from the tail up. He asked him what in the world he was trying to do - skin those fish like that. Bill told him that I had told him to do it that way. I told Gary that I had told him no such thing. Anyhow, it didn't matter. I went over and showed him how to do it right. He must not have cleaned very many catfish.

On another occasion Bill and I were up on Amistad in that same area and as we were cruising along, we began seeing a lot of swirls in the water close to the boat. I knew it had to be some kind of fish and most likely gars. I stopped and sure enough, we saw gars everywhere. I saw one over to the right about twenty feet and he had to be eight feet in length and as big around as I was. Made my hair stand on end. There were many that would weigh twenty to forty pounds. They must have been gathered there for spawning. It was an area of about a half-mile long.

I wished that we had had some snares tied to five-gallon jugs with some big chunks of jackrabbit on them.

THUNDERSTORMS SLIPPING UP ON US

Gary Kinnard and I went over to Lake Amistad to camp and fish. We were going to put the boat in up on the Pecos River. It was noon or after so we stopped at the north end of the Devil's River Bridge. We drove down below the bridge closer to the water and turned around facing north. We got in the boat as that was where our food was. We made sandwiches and were sitting there eating. After a while, we looked behind us and there was a rain shower coming our way not more than a hundred yards away. Well, before we could get things closed up and out of the boat, it was raining on us. We got soaked and so did our sandwiches. Did you ever eat a wet dripping sandwich? That one really slipped up on us.

We launched the boat at the Pecos River ramp. It's about a half-mile or so down to its mouth, where it runs into the Rio Grande. Going down lake there are some pretty high canyon walls on both sides of you. I guess we had gone a couple miles when all at once, there was a strong looking thunderstorm coming at us from the Mexico side. We decided to go back up lake about a mile and dodge into a slit in the wall on the Mexico side. By the time we got there, the storm had caught up with us and it got quite windy. As we went into the slit, the wind was doing funny things right there in the mouth of it. It was whirling and picking water up - in other words, it was raining up. It was kinda spooky looking. This reminds me of a story my Uncle Lester told me one time. He was a machinist in the Railroad Round House in Cheyenne, Wyoming, and he told of this workman who was watching a sight-glass that had oil dripping through it. Only thing, the oil was going up instead of down and the workman kept watching and finally said, "First time I ever saw a drop drip up." The line had steam pressure taking the oil up. I guess it would be something different. The oil was injected into the line just below the sight-glass.

After sitting the storm out, Gary and I went down to our favorite fishing spot.

ELEVATED SPOT IN THE WATER

In about 1988 Ron and Nancy came from Clarksville, Tennessee, to spend Christmas with us. Jim, Jimmy, Ron, and I planned an overnight trip to Amistad Lake. The day we went was awfully cold but we figured we were tough enough to take it. We hooked my boat on to the truck and headed out. We launched the boat at Diablo East boat ramp and headed out up lake. This ramp is in the Devil's River and it is three or four miles downstream before going into the Rio Grande. Turn up lake there and go for about ten miles to marker 14 where we took a due north course and went up Cow Creek. Cow Creek is a deep canyon going north and then branches into two creeks. When the lake is full, there is quite a lake in itself up in there. We had toured around up in there and then to camp, we came back out to the mouth of Cow Creek. There was a flat place pretty close to the water to put up the tent but it was wide open to the wind. Boy, was it cold. Those three guys slept in the tent and I slept in the boat. I put the top up and the side curtains on the sides and still just about froze. We did a little fishing but I think we got only one fish. Sleeping in the boat wasn't the best place in the world to sleep. The wind was slapping the waves against the boat and the boat banging on the rocks and besides, it was cold.

The next morning we decided to boat ride and not try any fishing. We went up lake to the Seminole Canyon, which was quite a few miles. The water had a little roughness to it but not all that bad. On the way back, Ron was piloting the boat and all at once he slowed and stopped and said, "What is that?" There was a place out from us about two hundred yards that looked elevated and the surface of the water was smooth. Also, there was a few birds flying and circling that spot and once in a while, one of them would dive into the water. In the winter, the spring water is warmer than the rest of the lake so fish come to live there and the bait fish are molested by the larger fish causing them to surface and the birds get after them.

After thinking about it for a minute, I said, "Wait a minute." I remembered that we had just passed marker 20 but not to 19 yet. I had a map in the glovebox I got out and looked at and sure enough, it showed the "Good Enough Spring" to be between markers 19 and 20 over on the Texas side. Ron maneuvered the boat onto the top of the elevated area and it would drift us away very quickly. The depth finder read 105 feet deep right in the middle of that place. That spring had to be putting out a tremendous amount of water to elevate the water like that.

I had seen the spring before; I remember when the lake was first being impounded, there was a floating marker there. Evidently the cable had broken and the marker went bye-bye to Mexico.

I talked to a fellow the last time I was over there and he said that he had been to that spring before the lake was formed and said it was quite a river coming down that canyon from that spring. I look for it every time I go by there now and you can see it even in pretty rough water. There will be a slick spot with no waves on it. It would be interesting to know where that water comes from. It would have to come from somewhere with a much higher elevation to have that much force.

TAKING TROTLINES UP IN A HURRY

Ruth and I went to Amistad Lake to camp and fish. The boat I had then was a tri-hull Glasstron with a 100-horse power outboard on it. I would take three six-gallon tanks of gas. One to go up lake on, one to run around fishing on, and the third to come back to the boat ramp. We put out three trotlines with about 30 hooks each and baited them. It was getting dark and we pulled into a little cove. We fixed something to eat and made our bed in the boat. We had seen lightning up in the northwest earlier and I told Ruth that we'll just about get rained on after while. Well, sure enough, just about midnight, thunder woke us up. For some reason, I thought we needed to get those lines up. We got the first one up and it began to rain. We'd sit under the top and wait and when it would let up a little, we'd go for the next one. After we got them all up, I began to think; why in the world did I think we needed to get those lines up? We weren't going anywhere - you couldn't go in the dark. Out on that big water, you can't see where you're going. A spotlight doesn't help. Ah, you might see a floating log or something if you were going slow enough. There is no way you could navigate except by compass and that wouldn't keep you from running aground. We went back to bed after the rain quit. Next morning we had no fish - no lines in the water - no fish. After breakfast, we trolled and got a few white bass and a few blacks. We did have fish for lunch that day. Had fun though, because we kept telling each other how much fun we were having.

RATTLESNAKE SCARE

I was out at the Rubyola farm about ten miles east of town doing some work for Bubba Day. The fields were grown up with huisache brush. Several years earlier some of the fields had been planted to giant Bermuda grass and some had buffel grass in them. The grasses were still where it wasn't choked out by the brush. I was shredding the fields and one day after I ate my lunch, I was laying on the ground greasing my shredder (I had to get on the ground in order to get to some of the grease fittings) when Bubba drove up and asked me if I had any drinking water. I told him I sure did - it's in the truck on the passenger side and for him to help himself. He got himself a drink and hopped back in his truck and took off. In a little while something caught my eye, which was about four or five yards from me. It was a rattlesnake and he was acting very strangely. He was rolling over and over and doing figure-8's and getting closer to me all the time. Of course at first, I thought Bubba had dropped him off there pulling a trick on me. Well, this rubbed me a little on the wrong side. That night I called him and told him I really appreciated him putting that rattler out there by me when he came after that drink of water. He asked me what I was talking about - he wouldn't do anything like that. I apologized. It was in the heat of the day and I guess the snake was having a heat stroke. After thinking about it, you never see rattlers moving around in the heat of the day. You'll see them late in the evening, at night or early in the morning. Of course he could have been stirred up from my shredding. It looked to me like he was headed to get under the shredder for shade. Anyhow, it was too close for comfort.

HAND ON RATTLESNAKE

I was irrigating at the farm using gated pipe. I turned the water on one morning and was adjusting the gates in the pipe. When the pipe is laid along the heads of the rows, you generally point the gates slightly below level. A lot of times, the pipe rolls over after the weight of the water gets in it and places the gates down low and sometimes they will be on bottom. Well, I was going along with my knees against the pipe and my upper body weight supported by my left hand on the pipe and adjusting the gates with my right hand. One can scoot along pretty quickly like this. Like I explained, some of these gates were pretty well on the bottom and as I was reaching under there I felt something with the back of my hand. I moved to the next opening and glanced back and I saw what I thought was a frog or a toad. I looked a little closer and it wasn't a frog or a toad at all - it was a rattlesnake. Boy, I'll tell you what, putting my hand against that rattler was a little too much for comfort. After that, I glanced ahead.

CAUGHT AT THE WRONG TIME

A few years ago I got a summons for Federal Jury duty. This summons was for a period of six months and the location was in Del Rio. I'd been called over three times and had never been chosen for a jury. My six months was just about up but I got called one more time.

Well, thinking I wouldn't be put on a jury this time either, I told Gary Kinnard and Bruce Ivey to hook onto my boat and come over and I would meet them at the bar-b-q place at noon. I'd be off and we'd go fishing for a couple nights out on Amistad Lake. They say, third time is the charm but this time; the fourth time hooked me. I got stuck on a jury.

I was able to meet those guys at the eating place at noon. I told them to go on out and put the boat in at Amistad Acres and I'd be out there a little after six that evening.

When you're on Federal Jury duty, you are required to wear a suit. I had not taken a change of clothes so I stopped by Wal-Mart and purchased a new tie - maybe I'd look a little different the next day.

I went on out to the Landing and they were waiting for me. I had changed my clothes there at the car so jumped in the boat with them and we took off to marker 14 and turned up Cow Creek. They already had the tent up so we fished until dark. Next morning after we ate, we fished a little and I got a nice 4-1/2 pound bass. We had to go 'cause we had a thirty-minute run to get to the car. I had to change clothes and get in to court by 9 AM so I had to trickle right along. I guess I had about 25 miles to drive.

I got back into court all right. We got through with the case mid-morning and I came on home. Gary and Bruce had said they were coming home that day, too, so I just let them have it.

A SLEEPING RATTLESNAKE

The old house at the farm needed a hole covered up to keep the owls out. The louver in the gable on the south end had fallen out and we were going to cover it with a piece of tin. The wind was blowing pretty hard so I decided to wait for a quieter day. I had taken a ladder out so I laid it down on the west side of the house out of sight of the road. I laid it on edge and leaned it against the house. A few days later we were out there and it was a nice quiet cold day so we decided to fix the hole. I walked around on the west side to get the ladder. I walked to about the middle of the ladder and reached down and took hold of it and right under my hand just the width of the ladder laid a great big rattlesnake. I mean not more than 14 inches from my hand. The snake didn't move when I moved the ladder. I told Ruth to bring my gun out of the truck. I pointed the gun and fired missing the head but going through the body. Man, you talk about a snake coming alive! He did! He began striking and hitting the ladder several times before I could get him killed. Apparently the snake had been asleep. It was a cold day and the sun was shining on that spot so I suppose he was basking in the warm sun.

The walls of the house were adobe construction with stucco finish. There was a hole down under the wall right there. A few days later, I went around to look in that hole and there was a snake down in it. I went back to the truck to get my gun but he was gone when I got back. No telling how many snakes lived under that old house.

NEARLY TOO DARK TO FIND CAMP

Around 1980, Bruce Ivey, Buddy Myska and I planned a fishing trip to Amistad Lake. Bruce and I went up and put in at the Pecos River Landing. Buddy was coming up the next day. Bruce and I had gone down lake some 12 miles and set up camp. We put out trotlines so had fish the next morning, and we did a little trolling so had a few other fish.

I guess Buddy got off work at five so he was pretty late getting up there. He brought gas for the boat, so we put that in and then he had to go park the car a half-mile up the hill. By the time we got back down to our fishing area, it was getting a little late and I couldn't seem to find the camp. There are so many coves and about dark, they all look pretty much the same. I realized then, one needs to put a marker that can been seen. One of those blockade flares or those blinking things would do. Of course, if it was good daylight, you may not be able to see it. Buddy had no idea where it was as he had never been there. We did find it - Bruce had begun to worry about us.

On another occasion, we three went to Amistad, but put in at Amistad Acres and went up Cow Creek. We camped closer to the mouth of the creek this time than we usually do. We decided to have a contest. We put $5 each in the pot. Right off, Buddy caught a real nice catfish - we were trolling too. Well, I figured he had the pot because we never get anything much that's very big. That afternoon, we decided to go up lake and try some other places. We followed the markers and I guess the lake lays mostly northwest to southeast but has several 90-degree turns, and two places I know of, it makes big "S" turns. In those two places you find yourself going south. Anyhow, at marker 19, I should have made a hard right but I forgot and went straight into Mexico. I knew I wasn't seeing anymore markers and wondered about it. After while, I thought I'd go to my right and get on the Texas side. We got to shore all right and later I realized we had gone into Mexico and had gone into a large bay and were at the edge of that. The lake was full and when it is, there is a very large area of water here. I mean miles of it. I most always look at my map and watch the compass. This time, I guess I was thinking about getting my money back.

We parked and Buddy got out of the boat and went one way to fish and I the other. I looked back toward the boat and Bruce was reared back fighting something (he had stayed in the boat) and then I noticed his rod got still. I went back to see if I could help. I could see brush under the water behind the boat so I knew what his trouble was. The fish had wrapped around the brush and now, you couldn't tell if it was still on or not. I told Bruce to go ahead and pull and break the line. Well, he couldn't break it - I couldn't either. I had a two-foot piece of 2 x 6 in the boat so I wrapped his line around it and pulled and guess what, I pulled the fish out of the brush. He began to run again and I was hollering at Bruce to keep the line tight. OK, but I still had his line wrapped around the 2 x 6. We had quite a time there for a little bit until I got his line off the board. He was letting the fish get under the boat and that was a no-no because of the danger of getting the line around the out drive of the boat. I took his pole and got the thing under control and then gave it back to him. By this time, the fish was playing out and he was getting it up to where I could net it. The fish was a 5-pounder and I knew Bruce had the pot now for sure.

After we returned to camp and realized where we had gone, Buddy and I started telling Bruce that his fish was illegal because he caught it in Mexico. Man, ole Bruce came unglued about that; he said there was no stipulation as to where the fish was caught. We said, yeah, it's just understood that it's not legal because you didn't have Mexico licenses. He said he didn't care, there were no stipulations and it was the biggest fish so far.

Next morning after breakfast we were walking along the shore fishing and I got a pretty good one on. I hollered at Bruce, "Looky here, I got one on and I think it bigger than yours!" It wasn't but I had Bruce watching pretty close.

We packed up our tent and gear and loaded in the boat getting ready to go and Bruce wanted his money. He said we were through fishing and he wanted the money right now. Ok, he got it. We stopped in Del Rio and ole Bruce set us up to a milk shake. I guess we all got a little of the winnings.

At home when we were around people we'd bring up this

thing about Bruce's illegal fish just to hear him holler. If we'd forget to say anything about it, he'd say something to remind us.

UPSET LITTLE RATTLESNAKE

I was out in a ranch planting deer patches one time. The rancher plants little acreages around over his ranch to oats for the hunters to have places to put up stands to watch for deer. I was planting with a big tiller and when I moved from one patch to another, I had to put the thing in road gear. I was in the process of changing the tiller, walking back and forth to the truck getting the tools I needed. All at once I noticed a small rattlesnake in my path just having a fit. I guess I must have stepped on him because he was really upset. Sure glad I had boots on. I've always heard that a bite from a small one is just as bad as from a big one. Considering it all, I have been very lucky not to have been bitten.

CA CA
THEY SAY THIS ROAD IS GOOD—BUT SOMETHING IS SURELY PULLING ME TO THE RIGHT IN THE REAR
DW

INTERESTING PLACES AND THINGS TO SEE ON THE WAY TO ALASKA

In 1997 Ruth and I, her brother, Kenneth, and his wife, Virginia, and Henry and Mary Ann Daly were heading to Alaska. Kenneth and Henry met at a roadside park near Junction and they spent their first night near Sweetwater. Ruth and I spent our first night in Lubbock visiting Benard, Cecil, Margaret, and their family. The next afternoon, we met the others at the Palo Duro Canyon Park.

We arrived at the Canyon and found the others. It was really nice down in there. There were a lot of clouds around and once, there was a park employee announcing there was a severe storm watch in effect. I don't even remember if it rained or not but it sure was cool and nice that evening and night. We all gathered at Ken's trailer for an evening feast - humm some good.

The next morning, we headed for North Platte, Nebraska. In the heat of the afternoon we were between McCook, Nebraska and North Platte, Nebraska, and Kenneth blew a tire on his trailer. We got that changed and made it on in all right. Ken's and Henry's stayed in an RV Park in North Platte and we went over to J. W. and Emma Jean's for the night. Emma Jean is my cousin.

Next morning, J. W. and I went to the city park there in town to look around. It is really a nice place. Lots of nice trees and a small lake with elk around here and there. There was a big bull and a couple cows laying in the water keeping cool. There were many kinds of ducks and geese around everywhere.

The thing that really interested me was their train engine display. There was a huge steamer there - really big. When we got in the cab, it looked like it was a hundred yards up to the front of that thing. You couldn't count the levers, valves, and gauges in the cab. Then of course, the conveyer that brought the coal from the tender to the firebox. However, this one could have been an oil burner. There was a large diesel unit there too. The engine was a large V 16 - the heads were off so you could see in there pretty good. Actually, the locomotive is electric. The big motor pulls a generator that furnishes the power to the electric motors that drive the thing. The first car behind this unit is a mail car - the U. S. postal people work here sorting mail to be delivered to the various towns and of course, they are picking up mail all along the way too. Behind the mail car is a baggage car for various types of baggage. If you are ever in North Platte, go to the city park and see this stuff. Also, North Platte, I think, is the largest railroad center in the country. I visited with a retired engineer (train driver) and he said that there were over one hundred trains coming in there everyday.

That afternoon we all headed west toward Cheyenne, Wyoming. Out in western Nebraska along I-80 there is a very large Cabela's Sporting Goods Mall. They have everything one could think of, and then some. If you're ever out there be sure and stop in - it's worth the while that you'd spend there. They even told us we could camp in their parking area. It wasn't quite camping time so we went several miles farther west and took an RV Park.

Next morning we came to Cheyenne and went into a place called Little America. We always buy the cheapest fuel of the whole trip right here in this place. We took I-25 north from here and near Buffalo, Wyoming, we changed roads and made it into Montana, stopping at a KOA Camp. There were no spots left but were permitted to park in the edge of a field for ten bucks. However, we did dump our rigs and fill up with water. That's worth something. This town was Harding, Montana.

We went west all the next day coming to Missoula, Montana, turning north a short distance out of Missoula heading toward Eureka, Montana. It was time to camp so we began looking for a place. A short distance north we saw a sign so turned in and found a very nice little camping park along the Jocko River. There was a bunch of ducks there in the park and Mary Ann got to feeding them bread. Boy, they really went for the bread and it was fun watching them beg for it.

Going north next morning we passed a beautiful lake (miles and miles of it) with many beautiful homes along its shores. Next big town was Kalispell and then to Eureka, Montana. Here, we turned west coming to Koocanusa Lake and going 23 miles down lake to where our friends, Tom and Terry Fatherree, were hosting a camp. It was really good to see them again and we met Henry's friends from Florida, George and Marge Wenten. We camped here two nights. Tom and Terry treated us to a nice fish fry and all the good stuff that went with it. The name of this camp was Peck Gulch. The main thing I remember about this place was the steep, steep road that led down to the camp from the main road. Fun though. My Dodge Diesel didn't seem to mind at all. Of course everybody else made it back up too. No problems.

The second morning, we four rigs lined up and headed north. We crossed into Canada without much ado. I think about the only problem we had at the border was that we couldn't take apples into Canada. Marge had several so we all filled up on apples and put the rest in the garbage before we could go.

A few kilometers on north we stopped at a fish hatchery. This was really interesting. You get to see the little bitty tiny fish with the yoke still attached to them - in fact, you see the yoke first. They have all the stages (sizes) all the way up to 10 pounders. The larger ones were outside in large tanks. Several kilometers more north we came to Old Fort Steel. This place is worth seeing - it seems to have been a complete little town with doctor's offices, churches, stables, farming equipment, a bakery, well, just all kinds of shops. There was a lot of old equipment there and the thing that interested me most was an old water wheel. The sign stated that this thing was in operation up until 1936. It was 36 feet in diameter with many water cups. The old generator that it pulled was there too. I never had thought about it, but I guess the wheel powered the generator and then the power it created was used for electric powered equipment. We remained in the parking lot here and had our lunch.

On north we began getting into the mountains and seeing a lot of beautiful scenery. We arrived at Lake Louise and parked in an RV Park for the night. We did drive up to the lake to look it over. The lake is fed by five glaciers and I tell you what, you don't see anyone bathing in this lake. You see a few of those little paddle wheel boats fiddling around in there. No one in the water though. There are two or three hotels there that you wouldn't believe. No telling how many rooms are in them.

Getting to the next place of interest the next morning was the Columbia Ice Fields. Here, there are all sorts of tours and ways to spend your money. You can take rides on the ice and walks too. You can drive fairly close to one and walk over to and on it if you like. The most interesting thing to me was the markers they had placed along the road going to the glacier, which indicated where it was in a particular year. The first one was 1924 and then one every five years there after. Really makes one realize how much and how fast the ice is melting. All these glaciers head rivers or calve into the ocean.

From here, we pointed our rigs toward Jasper. It's a beautiful drive with mountains on both sides of you. The country flattens out somewhat before reaching Jasper and we most always see game - elk and stone sheep. You quite often come up on stone sheep in the road. They seem to be feeding or licking something off the road. I've heard said it's the salt that is in the road material. Who knows, maybe they sprinkle salt in the road so the tourist will really think they are seeing something.

From Jasper, we headed west to Prince George where we fueled up and spent the night. The RV Park where we camped was beside a little lake and there were a few floatplanes moored in it. No flying going on, though.

Next, we head toward Dawson Creek, B.C. but turn off at Chetwynd to cut across and hit the Alcan just west of Fort St. John. We drove up the Alcan a few kilometers and stopped at a place named Pink Mountain. Here we fueled and took an RV Park for the night. Next morning I had gone to the dump to service the Airstream and just about then, it started raining and I mean we experienced a genuine bona-fide thunderstorm with plenty lightning and thunder! It rained as hard as I had ever seen it rain anywhere, anytime. It rained on us all that day. We got to a place where there was plenty of room for all of us to park in. I think it was an area where gravel had been taken but was level but pretty rocky. Here we spent the night. I'd been here before and have been there since. I think everyone was in their rigs eating and we heard someone holler, "Bull! Bull!" I looked out and there was a young caribou bull running around which was at least twice as big as our deer. He acted like he was wanting to get to a place and we were in his way. He ran around there long enough for everyone to get pictures.

Next day we headed toward Watson Lake, Yukon. Here is a city of signs. There are signs from every town and every country in the world I think. Someone said there were over 33,000 signs there. If you ever get up there, be sure to stop.

Next place is Whitehorse. However, we turned off at Jake's Corner and went to Carcross which is on the Skagway Road. Camped here and next day went down to Skagway. If the weather permits, this is one of the most beautiful drives one could ever make. Here you see Old Alaska and lot of people. If one of those big ships is in, the streets will be jammed. Fun though. Here, you can spend money all you want to. You can take air tours, chopper rides to the glaciers and get out and walk on them and then there is the train ride up over the White Pass. This is the famous pass where many men and mules and donkeys went up and over, back in the gold rush days. There were many animals and men too that lost their lives trying to make this pass. This little tour over, we went back up to Carcross for another night. There's a real nice museum here - don't miss it.

Now we are headed to Whitehorse where we fuel up and head on north to Dawson City, Yukon. On this stretch of road something happened that could have ruined the whole trip for us all. Henry went to sleep and ran off in a seven-foot ditch. Mary Ann said she wasn't asleep and said they really were airborn. George and I were up ahead and Kenneth was behind. Mary Ann came on the CB and said, "We're in the ditch but we are all right." Kenneth came on the CB and said, "No, they are not all right." He could see the cloud of dust they had made. George and I got turned around soon as we could and went back. Henry's suburban had four wheel drive and he was going to try to pull up that steep bank. I told him no, it was too steep - you'd turn over. If the suburban didn't turn over the trailer would have. Both tires were blown out on the right of his trailer and it surely would have turned over trying to come out of there. We finally talked him into going on down the ditch to a place that was not so steep. We got him up on the road and then we had to change both of those blown out tires. Henry had one spare and we used

Kenneth's spare. Both axles were bent and one enough to cause the tire to rub on the inside of the fender well, so we had to do something about that. He pulled it a little ways to a turnout and that is where we put our skills in operation. We put a jack under the middle of the axel and put most of the trailer's weight on it and then three of us got on the trailer's bumper and gave it the old "one-two-three" heave. Did the job - got it bent enough so the tire didn't rub anymore. Henry bought two new tires in Dawson City, so he'd have a spare now, and to replace Kenneth's too. We camped that night in a large turnout just after we crossed Willow Creek. (Who knows where that is?) I changed my fuel filter that evening. I had filled up with fuel back in Whitehorse and the transport was putting fuel in the underground tank as I was fueling. Right away, I noticed power failure. I figured I picked up a lot of sediment here. Going on to Dawson City next morning. We went up Bonanza Creek Road to the gold dredge. They all took the tour. Ruth and I did not as we'd done it a couple times before. I guess Virginia didn't either (they had done it before too). She made a birthday cake for Mary Ann and we had a little party for her when they came back from the tour. After the gold dredge tour, we took them to the place where they smelted the gold (earlier years) and visited the Machine Shop and the place where they generated their acetylene gas and made oxygen and bottled it. They used this for welding and cutting steel. There was all sorts of old equipment to look at. I think one of the most impressive things were the big "spuds" that were laying there on the ground. These things were about 20 feet long and 2 or 3 feet square and weighed several tons. Two of these spuds were used in that gold dredge to anchor it. These spuds were pressed down through the muck to bedrock to anchor the dredge. This creek was small but the dredge dug in front of itself creating a large enough place for the thing to float - it was moved by floating it. So you see why it had to be anchored. The tour guide said it took 20 years to go 8 miles. In this 8 miles, this thing moved many thousands of tons of rock. They dig down to bedrock (the gold is under all this rock and muck) and all this stuff goes through the shakers with water washing it as it shakes, and the gold ends up in the bottom trays. You got to remember that gold is 27 times heavier than water. The water here is recycled over and over and over. I guess you might say, water never wears out. They tell you many times over that you can't mine gold without water. All the rock coming out of the dredge is stacked behind. The tailpiece swings back and forth slowly - maybe 40 to 60 feet stacking the rock. When you see rock in this pattern, you know a dredge did it.

We spent the night in a RV Park in Dawson City. Everybody got all the looking done that they wanted so we headed on. First thing you do before going far, if you're headed to Alaska, is to cross the mighty Yukon River on a ferry. The river here must be a half-mile wide and is the muddiest water you ever saw. They have a dozer at both landings in case they have to be repaired. The ferry service is part of the highway system and there is no charge for its services.

Just a little about the Yukon River - they say it heads about 50 miles up from Whitehorse. Here it is a very clear water river and I'm sure it is clear on to its beginning. It flows northwest up to Fort Yukon, Alaska, and turns southwest to Russian Mission and then northwest up to Alakanuk and Emmonak, Alaska, where it empties into the Bering Sea. This river is in the neighborhood of 2,000 miles long. Can you believe that salmon come all that way to spawn in the headwaters of this mighty river? In Whitehorse there is a dam and there is a fish ladder up over it so the fish can get by and go on upstream to where they were hatched. They come back to spawn and then they die. There is a glassed area they have to come through and are counted and they can be trapped for viewing purposes. I have been there when they had some King salmon trapped and they are fairly good looking fish. Ah, they'll have some marks or scratches on them, but coming 1950 miles, they are bound to get into some scrapes.

Back to the road now. Leaving Dawson City, Yukon, crossing the river by ferry, you go up on The Top of the World Highway. This road is a dirt road but is well maintained and is an enjoyable drive. As the name of the road indicates, you are on top looking down on both sides and much of the time, it is above timberline. This country is not rugged like the Colorado mountains. It's smoother looking. The timber is not big stuff. In fact, I don't think the timber is even used for anything. Some times you see patches of smoke - fires started by lightning. This road takes you into Alaska at the most north entry of the state by road. Its name is Poker Creek. Some miles into the state, we pulled off the road to camp. There was plenty of room for everyone. Kenneth changed the oil in his truck and greased his wheels, I think. He said he wanted them to roll easy. Ok, I'll go for that.

Next day, we roll into a place called Chicken. There is a Post Office and of course a place to spend money if you have any left. The road from here is a winding one and lots of ups and downs. There is a place of interest - an old dredge setting there almost rotted away. There is a lot of the old iron machinery such as winches still in it. It's been many years since this one was used. There was a little stream of water where it sat.

Our next stop was Tok Junction, Alaska. Tok is on the Alcan and a good place to fuel up and wash your rig if you want. We visited the large visitor center here and one can get just about all the information you would ever need. From here we head southwest making it to Glen Allen where George replaced a tire and we all took an RV Park for the night. Did laundry here too.

Next morning on our way, we stopped at a musk ox farm near Palmer. Ruth and I had been there twice before so we set this one out and waited for the others. Leaving here, we motored toward Anchorage. In Anchorage, we go to Tom and Terry's daughter and son-in-law's machinery yard. They are in the paving business and have this nice place to stay. There is a place to service our rigs and wash them - just about anything you need to do. There is a nice shower inside with plenty of hot water (you need lots of it up there, believe me) that we had access to. Really a nice place to rest up a couple days and go shopping if we needed to. I had told Henry and George we were going to park here and if they didn't want to, they could go to a park somewhere. I couldn't believe they wouldn't want to park here. After we pulled in and they looked it over they decided they didn't want to stay there. I'd been telling Henry all along what we were going to do and if they didn't care to do that, feel free to do something else. They went to an RV Park that evening and the next day they went on down to the place where we were going to do our halibut fishing. I had told Henry how to find the place. He called me two mornings later and said they were going out for halibut that day. I told him we were coming on down that day and would see them when they got back from fishing. When they came in, they had some fish all right. I asked him if he was going to can some of it. He said he didn't have a cooker. I got mine out and loaned him some jars and helped him pack the jars and showed him what to do about the cooker. Next morning, he did another cooker full. He told us that he and George didn't want to fish anymore - not even for salmon - that they were going on. Kenneth, Virginia and I went out the next day. She got one weighing 118 pounds and Kenneth got one tipping the scales at 87 pounds. I caught four small ones and got to keep the two I wanted. The last place we dropped anchor I got onto something heavy. The thing was paying my line off the reel and the captain would keep tightening the tension until he was afraid to tighten anymore. Finally I could hold it and gain a little bit once in a while. Little by little I was gaining on this thing that I thought was a "barn door." I don't know how long it took me to get him up. The captain got his shotgun and harpoon ready. When I got it up to where we could see it, guess what, it was a big stingray. The captain said that I didn't want that and was about to cut the line. I said I didn't know but I did want a picture of it. He left it on the line long enough for me to get a snapshot and then he took the hook out and let it go. When we got back to camp, I told George about my stingray and he said, "Yeah, they take those wings and cut scallops out of the thin part - expensive platter." I thought I had heard that before. The captain just didn't want to mess with a stingray - we were halibut fishing. We were fishing 175 feet deep so you see one reason why it took so long to land a fish. When you pull the line up to check the bait, it's quite a chore with that 4-pound lead on it. I thought sure I was going to put Virginia and Kenneth in the shade. Ha Ha, the joke was on me. Well, anyway I had caught four and got to keep the two I wanted. Two is the limit. We stuck around this camp the next day canning fish. We put several packages in our little freezers to use fresh. I mentioned the captain getting his shotgun ready - they always kill any fish over 40 pounds before bringing them on board. The things can break your leg if let flop around on deck and you happen to get in his way. We have fished with these people three times and will go back again if and when we get back up there. Their business name is "Heavenly Sights."

From here we went to Morgan's Landing on the Kenai River to fish for Sockeye salmon, known as "red" salmon. After fishing here three days we went back to Anchorage for a couple days and rested up.

After we rested up we went over on the west side of the Cook Inlet to the Little Susitna River to fish for Silver salmon. We got Silvers, Chums, and Pinks here - a total of nine fish.

From here, we went to Denali Park and took the tour of the park all the way back to Wonder Lake - some 75 miles to the lake. This is an all day bus ride. We took our lunch and drinks - no place to buy anything in the park. We always see game. Caribou, Dall Sheep, Goats, Moose, Bear, and Arctic Fox, and once we saw three Timber Wolves. You also see lots of chipmunks and ground squirrels. Ruth and I have taken this tour four times and may do it again - if and when.

From here we go to Fairbanks and camp 12 miles north at a place called Fox.

Next morning we venture north following the "haul road" which will take us to the Artic Circle and farther if you like. Two years before, we and Kenneth and Virginia did go all the way to Dead Horse and took a tour to Prudhoe touring the oil producing area and "mile 0" of The Great Pipeline and they took us to the Arctic Ocean where we only felt of the water. Said we could go bathing but after finding out the water temperature was 34 degrees - ha - no thank you. The wind was coming off that water pretty strong and we considered it cold wintertime for us. I might add, this was in late July, too.

I'll get back to the current trip. Also, on this trip I was pulling a 29-foot Airstream trailer - think I mentioned it before. Anyway, we had gotten a hundred or so miles up and Kenneth called me on the CB and told me that I had lost my sewer hose holder from off the rear of my trailer. It was a good thing he was behind me. The first turnout we came to, we pulled out so I could tie the thing back on. Well, here comes two vehicles turning in there from the north. Lo and behold, it was Henry and George. They had gone north as far as Coldfoot, spent the night there and were returning. They had planned to drive all the way to Dead Horse but George had left his medicine in his motor home back in Fairbanks. I think, after they had to pay well over a hundred and twenty-five dollars each for a room in Coldfoot it discouraged them. They would have had to pay that or more up at Dead Horse and then again at Coldfoot on their way back. Anyway, while visiting, Henry started telling me about this little souvenir he had bought for himself. Ole George started laughing when Henry said he had paid 35 bucks for this little oolu. (This is a knife that is rounded about 5 inches wide with a handle on top of it) I really don't think it is very practical - just something to sell. Then I told them that I had bought myself a little something too. I bought this fillet knife down at Ninilchik and paid $80 for it. Virginia spoke up and said, "No Dale, you paid $85 for it." Then I said, "Yeah, it's better than I thought." Well, old George liked to have cracked up on this one. We bid each other goodbye and went our separate ways.

I don't remember where we camped that night. We crossed the Yukon River - the bridge is much higher on the south side than it is on the north. The terrain is higher on the south so the bridge is slanted down. The pipeline is suspended on the side of the bridge. On the north side of the river is a big camp and service station. We fueled here. The Arctic Circle is about 60 miles north of the river. We stopped here for pictures and visited with other people doing the same thing. We went about 30 miles more to the north to where we camped for three nights. We were by the Jim River and this is where we fish for Arctic graylings. I was having some kind of problem with my Airstream - the bottom trim was popping off (rivets pulling through) so I spent a half day putting that back on. It seemed like the right rear was sagging but couldn't tell why. I also changed oil in my truck and greased 'er up. Oh yeah, when turning off the main road to come here to camp, I noticed as I looked in my rearview mirror that my left rear tandem on my trailer was about flat. I stopped right there and put a plug in the very obvious hole. I had an air compressor so there was no problem in airing it up. Fixed it good 'cause it rolled me all the way home.

We hadn't been there long, I think the next day; here came an outfit with an airboat and a bunch of people with cameras and stuff. They put the boat in the river and began tearing up and down the river - they just about slung all the water up on the banks. As Kenneth and I stood there watching, a guy came over and told us that we would be on NBC television next Monday night. We told him that wouldn't do us any good; we wouldn't be around a TV then. These pipeline people were doing a demonstration on cleaning up an oil slick should one ever occur in any of the rivers along the pipeline. After it was all over and they all left, there was a pipeline man who came back to see if there had been any trash left around there. We talked to him and he told us where he thought we could catch some fish. He said to go back to the main road, turn left and go a little past the pump station on our right and go down a road to the left. We would get to their water well and to stop there and go on a trail to the river. He said he always got fish there. Well, we did that the next morning and sure enough, we got some fish. When we first got there, Kenneth went downstream of me about 150 yards out on a gravel bar. I heard him holler at me and when I looked, there was a cow moose that had come to the river between us. I think she was going to cross or wanted to cross on that gravel bar Kenneth was on.

After we got enough of the Jim River, we went back to Fox and took the same RV Park. We called the gold mine nearby and made reservations to tour it. This mine was very interesting; they gave the history of prospecting, early power machinery and modern mining. They gave all of the tourists a little sack of gold bearing dirt. They had rows of water troughs and gold panning pans and everyone panned for gold. Everybody was supposed to get a little gold and I think they did. Ruth's and mine together was about $7.00 worth. They had scales there so you could have it weighed. They also had plenty of little gadgets you could buy to put your gold in. Ruth said she heard one woman trying to trade her gold for one of the gadgets. That didn't work. They had all sorts of refreshments in this gift shop and it was on the house - included in the ticket. A very enjoyable tour.

Back at camp, we did repairs on Kenneth's trailer. He replaced the shackle bushings - had to have a little lathe work done on the new ones he bought in order for them to fit. Also, it was a good thing that I had an air compressor and an air wrench. One of those bolts we would never have gotten off without it.

In the park office I saw an ad on fly-in fishing. Kenneth said they'd do it, so I called this guy. He said he couldn't come out unless he had four people to go but if we'd go this evening, he would take us three because he had to go get some people out there anyway. I told him all right and he told me we needed to be there about seven that evening and be ready to go. Bob Elliot was his name and he lived close to the Paddle Wheel Boat Port on the Shena River. His plane was moored right there by his house. He put our gear in the pontoons (floatplane) and we climbed in and he fired her up and away we went. His plane was a Cessna 205 with a turban engine with a three bladed prop. I asked him how many horsepower he had. He said "410". He took us out west of Fairbanks about 60 miles to the Mento Flats. He showed us from the air where to fish - in the channels between the swamps. We saw moose and a Trumpeter Swan in the flats too. He had a cabin out there with bunks and a little cooking gear and there were three small boats with 3 HP Honda outboard motors on them. Plenty of gas and an LP gas stove in the cabin. Only thing wrong - just one - the wind was blowing like crazy when we got there and blew the whole time we were there. He dumped us out and picked up three that were waiting to come back. It was about 9 o'clock PM. Kenneth and Virginia took one boat and I another. It was hard to fish and operate the boat because of the wind. Anyhow, I fished until midnight - it was getting pretty dark. I had gotten four Northern Pike but was so tired, I turned three of them back figuring I could get my limit next day. We got out pretty early and the wind was still just as strong so I decided to walk. I walked up and down those channels casting in them and got only one strike the whole morning. After lunch, I took a boat and went fishing. Like I said, it was hard to operate the boat and fish, too, because of the wind. Well, finally I got one on so I tossed the anchor out so I wouldn't have to worry about the boat. I got the fish landed. I tell you what, you don't put your fingers in a pike's mouth - they got teeth like you wouldn't believe. I sat right there and caught the rest of my limit. He said we could bring only five fish home but he didn't say how many we could eat while there. We fried fish twice while there and then brought our five each home. I went back to the cabin with mine and Kenneth and Virginia were there too. We filleted all our fish and packed our gear and waited for Bob - he came about 7:00 like he said he would. He took us back in and we went back to camp where Ruth was waiting. I really enjoyed that trip. Would have been much better had the winds been calm. You can't win them all, however.

Next morning we didn't rise very early - we needed a little rest from all that fishing. We pulled out shortly after noon and the next night, we camped in an RV Park in North Pole, Alaska. North Pole is only a short drive on the Alcan southeast of Fairbanks.

We followed the Alcan coming out of Alaska into the Yukon all the way to a short distance northwest of Watson Lake, Yukon, where we turned down the Cassiar Highway. This is called the alternate route. Somewhere down the line on this road we turned into a turnout and I told Kenneth I wanted to elevate the trailer up on blocks so I could get under it and find out what my trouble was. The inside had begun to smell strong of sewer so I needed to find out if there was anything I could do. I backed the trailer up pretty high on blocks and we got under and found that the frame on the right rear behind the axles was broken. There wasn't anything at all we could do except try to take it easy on the bumps. Down this road some 350 miles we go back into the southeastern tip of Alaska to a town called Hyder. If you ever drive to Alaska, by all means go to this place either going up or coming back. If the weather permits, you will view one of the most beautiful drives in the world. You pass several kilometers right in the bottom of a gulch and will see glaciers on both sides and several waterfalls. This drive is in B.C. but soon you enter Alaska. By the way, we ran into Henry and George again here in Hyder. They were dining - we saw their rigs and stopped and they came out to visit a short while. We planned to fish some here but they told us fishing was going to be closed because the ice dams had broken up in the glaciers and had flooded the canal that the Salmon River goes into and pushed all the fish back toward the ocean two weeks. That was verified when we talked to some game department people a little later. So, we didn't spend much time here if we couldn't fish, so we headed out of there. We went back 40 miles to get on the Cassier Highway again in British Columbia and going south for a hundred miles and coming out on the Yellow Head Highway and headed toward Prince George and camped there that night. We had originally planned to head to Washington State and come down into California to visit the Redwoods and we had to make up our minds by the time we arrived in Prince George. Kenneth said, "Maybe since your trailer is broke, maybe we better head on home the shortest way." I agreed with him. Leaving Prince George we went back the same way we had come up. To Jasper, to Lake Louise and then a little east to Calgary and south coming into Montana at Sweet Grass. We camped at least two nights in Montana and the next night we camped in Cheyenne, Wyoming. Here at this RV Park, I tried to buy a slide-in pickup camper. We couldn't get together on the price. Leaving Cheyenne, we went down to Mantoth Springs, Colorado. We took an RV Park. The next morning we went up Pike's Peak via the cog rail. This trip wasn't so good - the weather was closed in all the way up and all the way back. We checked out of the Park shortly after noon and headed south on I-25. We pulled into a roadside park and had our lunch. The clouds were building and looking very angry and it wasn't long until we were running in the rain. From Raton Pass in New Mexico over to Clayton, we were in very heavy rain. We ran out from under the clouds a little while before getting to Clayton. We took a KOA camp here and just barely got set up and it caught up with us. Rained like the dickens for a little while and then it calmed down for the night.

Going through Lubbock that day, I stopped and called the

salesman whom I was dickering with on the slide-in camper - to try to deal with him again. He told me that I didn't have to worry about that camper anymore, it was sold. I thanked him. We went down to Sweet Water and went into an RV Park for the night. The next day we made it home without incident.

I bet I wasn't home twenty minutes when the phone went off and guess who it was? It was that salesman telling me the guy who had bought the camper couldn't get the money so it was still available. I made an offer including installing an air conditioner in the camper. We closed the deal on the phone. Of course I agreed to send some money right away which I did. We went up to Cheyenne to get it in a couple weeks or so.

Here at home, I put the Airstream up on blocks high enough that I could work under it. I had to take off the under skin in order to work on it. The channel iron frame was broken on the bottom and cracked up the side. I had to cut a portion out where it was buckled and then slice the channel with the torch and straightened it out pretty well. I welded that all up and then bridge braced it and then I did the other side the same way so it would look the same. I had just barely gotten this done when Ed told me his friend whom he goes to West Texas hunting with was looking for an old Airstream. They came the next day to look. I told them what had happened and what I had done and told them to look it over. Luther said he didn't know anything about it - if I said it was fixed, that was good enough for him. His friend Rex got under it and looked and I guess liked it all right. Anyway, Luther gave me a check for what I was asking for it and they pulled it off down the road. I got my money out of it and I was real happy about that. I think Ed said they have pulled it out to West Texas the past three years so I guess it is serving well. I think, as far as my repair job worked, it'll serve.

Ruth and I went to Alaska using our newer camper in 1998 and plan to go again this year, in 2000.

1998 TRIP TO ALASKA WITH A COUSIN

On a Christmas card for 1997 to my cousin who lives in Gaylord, Michigan, I asked her if she and her husband would like to drive to Alaska with us the following summer. She wrote back and said that sounded good but they had their summer already planned. Well, it wasn't long until she called and said that they just might do that. Later on she called and said that they were going to drive up even if for some reason, we didn't. By this, I knew she was hooked. We talked back and forth pretty often. She wanted some ideas on how to prepare for the trip. I told her she needed to can some meat and beans - told her about what we did. I don't think she ever canned stuff before, but she got busy and bought meat when she could catch it on sale and put it up. Worked out real well.

We planned to meet at a campground near Eureka, Montana, that Tom and Terry Fatherree were hosting that summer. Juanita and Kenny were going to a family reunion in Wyoming a few days before we were to meet - worked out just right.

We rolled out a couple mornings later going into Canada and making the same stops that we had made the year before. Of course we had seen all these things but they hadn't; but we were willing to wait so they could do these things. We camped in the same places until we got up above Chetwynd, B. C. Juanita had studied the Mile Post a little closer than I. She wanted to visit two dams on the Peace River. The first one offered self-tours with a lot of information - it was all right too. The other one was the Bennett Dam. This was really nice. It was very educational in that it had a science area with all sorts of ways electricity could be generated. There were machines to crank, things to pump, things to rub together - really interesting. One machine would light a bulb and then two bulbs, and a good bit faster, the TV would come on. If you could make the TV come on, they'd give you a pen. Course we got a pen anyway. Then, they took us on a tour. We boarded a bus that took us down inside the dam. Then we walked down to where the turbines and generators were. We saw where the water came out of the turbans and went into the conductors that took it back into the river below. This was a very interesting tour and it was free. Do it if you ever get up there – it's worth while. We camped in an RV Park in a nearby town by the name of Hudson Hope, B. C. This camp was free, too, but had a kitty in case you wanted to donate. Worth something to service your RV. Right?

Another place we'd passed by several times before, several miles or kilometers up the road, was a place that was tropical. It never freezes there in winter because of the hot springs all in the area. There are many tropical ferns and all sorts of plants growing there. Many animals congregate here in winter and that means the bears come too to prey on the others and it becomes very dangerous. In fact, not too long ago, we saw on TV where a woman was killed by a bear sometime back.

We had gone about a month earlier this time because I wanted to fish up in the Arctic first. One of the pipeline workers had told Kenneth and me the year before there would be less water in June than in July. Don't kid yourself, Dale, there was more water. We did eat fish though - in spite of it all.

The rest of the trip was about the same as the others. Mostly, we fished and camped. The story before this one gave much more detail pertaining to our activities

Juanita and Kenny left before we did - they were going back down the west coast to Vancouver to visit some of their children. On our way home, Ruth and I came down through North Platte, Nebraska, to visit some of our folk. We found the weather to be much warmer here than in Alaska - downright HOT!

BEAUTIFUL SIGHTS

We hadn't been home very long after returning from our 1998 Alaska trip that Kenneth and Virginia suggested we go out to North Carolina to see the fall leaves. We had worn our tires pretty thin but we decided we'd like to do that.

We planned our trip for the second week in October. However, Kenneth said he would call out there to a tourist bureau or somebody who would know when the best time would be. About a week before we planned on leaving, he called out there and they informed him that we should come a week later. Said the weather hadn't been cold enough yet to turn the leaves their fall colors. Ok, we then planned to go a week later.

Nancy, our older daughter who lives in Clarksville, Tennessee, had bought an Ivers & Pond grand piano from Ruth's sister Lee. The first night of our trip would be spent in San Marcos at her house. We loaded the piano in back of Kenneth's truck to haul it. He was pulling a trailer so his truck could also be loaded. I had a slide-in camper in my truck so couldn't haul it in mine. Lee had mustered two helpers and Larry came and brought the dolly and with the help of everyone, we got it loaded, packed, tied, and talked to and tarped with padding under the tarp. Lee had prepared a big ole pot of stew to eat after the work was done. We spent the night in her yard and after breakfast next morning, we were off to Tennessee.

We spent one night on the road and late the next evening we arrived in Clarksville. Nancy had the helpers lined up to unload that evening but she called us on our mobile and said she sent them home and that we would do it in the morning. Next morning, four big strong guys came and with Ron's supervision, they got it off the truck and on the mover and into its resting place. We put the legs on it and let it be. I was "the old man" so I got to watch.

Kenneth had experienced some kind of trouble with his trailer brakes just before we got to Nancy's so he undertook to fix that problem the next day. He thought once, it was the brake control, but then decided no. You know, we piddled with those things all day - he finally rewired or changed some of the wiring and finally decided he had the brakes working.

The next day was Sunday so we went to church with Nancy and Ron and Caleb - their grandson. She is the choir director of a church in Elkton, Kentucky, about 35 miles away.

Ok, next morning we pulled out. Didn't go far though - the first turn to the left from the house, Kenneth noticed his trailer brakes pulsing when he signaled left. I told him it had to be fixed so let's go back to Nancy's where there was a good concrete driveway to park and work on. He had thought it was the control at one time so we went to an RV supply and bought a new one. That was the trouble. Now, of course, we had to put the wires all back like they were before. Like I have said before, you can't win 'em all. One is supposed to learn from their mistakes.

On the road for sure now, we got a little past Knoxville and pulled into an RV Park for the night. The next morning we went down to Gatlinburg and down into North Carolina and got on the Blue Ridge Parkway. The road took us right up into the mountains and everything turned red. I couldn't believe how the color changed - breath taking. Going along taking in the beauty and all at once you realize the predominate color is orange and then in places, it turned yellow. Let me tell you, God's world is beautiful. Tell you something else; we'd be in a yellow area and there is a bright red tree stuck in there. Talk about something catching your eye, that did. In several places it seemed we were on top of the world and could see several ridges of mountains in the distance and it looked like blue smoke covered the distant ones. We spent one night up on the ridge in a park and I tell you what, it did cool off. The next morning, we went to Ashville and visited a large craft and art display market. There was a lot of beautiful stuff there - we found out about "up-town" prices too. When afternoon came, we decided to head back to Clarksville. We got out of the mountains and spent one night on the way to Nancy's.

Back at Nancy's and Ron's for the weekend. Ron took us fishing in Barkley Lake which is an impoundment on the Cumberland River. We got a few fish - one real nice catfish. We went to church with them again on Sunday.

Come Monday morning, we were on the road again heading west to Springfield, Missouri. Here we visited Bass Pro Shop. This is a large sporting goods complex. There is a nice museum there with most all of wildlife's creatures. If you have any money left, it's not hard to get rid of it here. Later in the day, we went down to Branson, Missouri. Here you can see all sorts of TV shows and spend all the rest of your money. We spent the night here in an RV Park.

Next day we made it to Eureka Springs, Arkansas. We found an RV Park fairly near the theater where the Great Passion Play takes place. We attended the play that night. Actual play time is about two hours. About four hours adding "go and come."
Next morning, we went to the theater in daylight. It's quite a place. I wanted to see how they took Jesus up in the air. There was a cable stretched overhead and then a hoist that lifted him up into the air supported by that cable. Real effective at night with the light shining on his white garments.

From Eureka Springs, we journeyed south to Fair Field Bay, Arkansas to visit Ronny and Kathy Waycaster. He was pastor here at our church at one time. When we arrived in town, I called him at the church and he came to us and led us back to the church. They were serving a meal at the church that Wednesday evening so we got invited to eat. Good stuff. We attended their prayer service after the meal. We spent the night in the church parking lot and Ronny came the next morning and led us to their house. Boy, he fixed a King's breakfast for us. I told him I'd stay longer if he'd do that every meal. He said he sure would. Getting to his house was quite a thing; up and down hills and roads leading everywhere. I asked him if he'd ever gotten lost trying to get to the house. He said yeah, once. I bet you could have lots of fun in those hills when an icy spell was in progress.

When we got ready to go, Ronny led us out and put us on the road to Little Rock. The drive down through the Ozarks to Little Rock is a very pretty one. Here, we got on the main drag going toward Dallas. We had just gotten off this Interstate to go down to Canton and Kenneth ran out of gas. He was pouring his spare gas into his truck when a lady stopped and told us there was an RV Park just ahead about a mile. We told her that's what we are looking for - she said her husband was there in the office. OK, we parked there for the night. There was a nice lake on their property so I got my casting rod out and did a little plugging. I got one pretty nice bass. Just one so I put him back.

Next morning we went on to Canton where the big Flea Markets are. We paid money to get in on the grounds. Three dollars I think but that gave us all day parking and then Ruth and I spent the night too. Kenneth and Virginia's daughter met us there that afternoon so they went back with her to Arlington and spent the night there. Ruth and I headed south next morning and found the drive to Waco a very nice one with a good bit of color. From Waco, we followed I-35 down to Moore where we head southwest on 57 and 83 at La Pryor going south to Crystal City.

We were home again from another nice trip. In a couple days after unloading the camper, we took it out to Ed's place and put it under the shed. The sun never hits any part of it nor does the rain ever get on it. That should prolong its life.

SHEAR PIN FAILS

Henry Daly and I and our wives planned a river trip. He and I decided to make a run through the river the day before just to see how things were as far as fallen trees in the way and logjams. We found the river to be fairly open and the water running strong. I had a new motor - one of those water-cooled exhaust air-cooled engines. It was a single and vibrated pretty bad but had good power. I think I sheared one pin on that run. We made it through there in 3 hours that day - that's moving on down river.

Next day we packed up. My boat was a 14-foot flat bottom and I had this new motor - a Sears 7 1/2 horse power thing. It had the shear pin system with no rubber cushion in the prop. So, that meant when the prop hit something solid, it sheared the pin. This system is hard to tolerate when you've been used to the other kind. Henry's boat was a 12 or maybe a 10-footer - pretty little. His motor was a 5-horse power Johnson which was real nice for that size boat.

Ruth and I were in the lead a little ways. We came to a place where the water was swift and went under a drift so you had to make a quick right turn in order to keep from hitting the drift. We made it all right and then we pulled up below there and waited for Henry and Mary Ann. When Henry came into it, he crashed right into the drift. Well, they managed to get out of the boat but were close to the other side so they got out on that side. They couldn't get up that bank because it was a caved off place and straight up. I had gotten their boat out all right and was helping Mary Ann get across that swift water. It was about hip deep and swift and was hard to stand in, much less walk in. She kept saying, "I'm not scared, I'm not scared." I told her she ought to be scared; if the water swept her off her feet she would end up under that drift of trash that was hung on a grapevine. Got her to safety and then I pitched Henry a rope and helped him across as he hung onto the rope.

There was another place we had a problem. Closer to the Evans Lake Ruth and I went into a place that was swift and narrow and on the right bank there was a stool of willow trees.

This clump of willows was kinda laid low out over the water and somehow, we got side ways in that place and here came Henry and Mary Ann and rammed us right in the side. His boat went up over the side of mine but I was able and strong enough to get it off very quickly. I think if I hadn't gotten his boat off me as quick as I did, we both would have capsized - our left side would have gone under and he would have gone under stern first.

Miraculously, we made it to the Evans Lake. We made camp - we both had tents. We got our kitchen set up - we had a folding table and stools, gas stove and lantern. We set out three trotlines and went back and ate supper and then went back and baited our lines. Next morning we harvested the fish. Plenty to eat anyway.

The second night about the time we went to bed, it came up a genuine thunderstorm. It rained like you wouldn't believe. The river came up several inches and there was lots of trash washed off the banks. By next day, the water had cleared up. We did pretty good on the catfish - brought several home.

The last day there, I asked Mary Ann to make some of her famous fish soup. She did and I was surprised, it was really good. She cut the fish up in little squares and boiled it along with several veggies - I know we had potatoes and onions and maybe she put some canned veggies in - whatever, it was really good.

The morning after the third night, we took our trotlines up and packed up and headed down river. We hadn't gone far before I sheared a pin - I thought. I took the prop off and the pin wasn't broken at all. It had ground the gears up in the foot. Now, Henry had to tow me. His little 5-horse motor did a pretty good job of it, too. Wasn't too fast but sure beat paddling. Every time we went through a rapid I'd turn loose of the towrope. We got through most of them fairly well. The water was running strong enough that we didn't have to get out very often. After getting home a day or two later, I took the motor down to Sears and told Victor Malto I didn't want it. He said that they'd fix it for me and I said that I knew they would but I didn't want it if it was going to grind the gears up ever once in a while. It needed stronger gears or a smaller shear pin.

A FISH STORY

Ruth and I have been through the river together several times and I always was telling her about getting into the crappie and catching them as fast as you could bait your hook. I don't think she believed me 'cause I never could prove it to her.

This time we came into the Evans Lake, we fished right at the upper end of the big water where there are a bunch of old logs and we caught several Warmouth perch. Some call them goggle eye because of the red ring around their eyes. Then we went down closer to the lower end and made camp. After while, we decided to go back up there and try for more goggle eye when I saw a twig sticking up out of the water about a hundred yards from camp. I stopped and tied to it and we started catching crappie just like I had told her. She said, "I believe you now." We got 25 and I decided to start cleaning them. I cleaned the first one and threw the head and other stuff overboard and the fish stopped biting right then and that was it. I went ahead and finished cleaning them, and then we went back to camp and had a fish fry. We had set out a couple trotlines so we went about dark and baited them. One line was down from camp a little bit and the other was about 75 or 100 yards up above the crappie hole. Next morning we had several catfish for our efforts. One thing I noticed was; one of the fish that we caught up above the crappie hole had a large lump in his stomach I noticed when I cleaned it. I cut it open and it was one of those crappie's heads.

After we ran and took up our lines, we went back to camp and Ruth fixed breakfast while I cleaned the fish and then we packed up to leave. I said, "Let's go and try the crappie hole a little while." Ok, we did and we got 19 more nice ones. Ruth said again, "Guess I believe you."

A SURE SPOT FOR CRAPPIE

I spoke of a crappie hole in the Evans Lake in an earlier story. We had found a submerged oak tree that produced crappie.

That summer I must have come through there at least 10 times. The water was running nicely and there were very few things you had to look out for. Enough water that you could go right over the rapids - just wasn't any trouble at all. We'd always stop at our crappie tree. On the way down, we'd stop and catch minnows so we'd have bait. Finally one time, the twig was gone. The tree had melted down enough that you couldn't see the thing. Well, I had noticed when I'd been there before, just how the trees up on the banks looked. So I got spotted according to my landmarks and dropped a line with a hook on it down and got it caught on some brush and set it real good and tied a bobber on it. We got our fish all right. Before we left, I tied the bobber to where it was a half foot or so under the surface so other people wouldn't see it. That worked for several times – well, the rest of the times we came through that summer.

Rosemary, our daughter, and son-in-law, Larry, wanted to come through. She wanted to fish but Larry said he wanted to see the scenery - didn't care about fishing. Ok, we loaded up and went to the river. On the way down to the Evans Lake we got our minnows and soon arrived at our crappie tree. Rosemary and I were catching fish right along and in a little bit, Larry spoke up and said, "I want to catch a fish." I gave him my pole and line and he put it down and came up with a fish pretty quick. He sat there and caught several and I think he really enjoyed doing it.

We could fish there at the lake until 5 o'clock and with the river flowing good and being free of fallen trees, we could be at the landing in a couple hours.

COLD WET TRIP DOWN THE RIVER

The time was late winter or maybe we should say, early spring. We were having cold fronts pretty regularly. Seems like the north wind would blow for a couple days then a couple days of open weather and then the clouds would return and then we'd have drizzle a day or so. Ruth and I decided to start down the river while the north wind was still blowing; then most of the trip would be dry.

The first night we camped at the lower end of the Kingfisher Hole. I always thought that place ought to be a good place to set lines for catfish. There was a nice little knoll on the west side of the river to put our tent. We seined for minnows and got enough to bait our lines. We had gotten one crawfish and we put it on a line just across from our tent. I told Ruth that I bet we'd get a cat on that one. We got up once in the night and ran our lines and we got two or three fish. Nothing on the crawfish, however. Next morning I looked to see if the crawfish line was moving and sure enough, it was. We got a nice channel cat on it.

It was cold that morning - steam was rising off the water a great deal. The air was so much colder than the water, causing the vapors to rise. We took the rest of our lines up and headed on down river.

The second night we camped close to the upper end of the Evans Lake. We set our three trotlines and baited them late in the evening. We used mostly cut bait this time along with some live minnows. We got up in the night to run our lines and when we started to rebait we discovered the raccoons had gotten in the boat and ate up the bait that we had in a can under the seat. So much for that idea.

In the morning, early before daylight, rain woke us up. I was really surprised. I really thought we'd have some open weather after the north wind, but we didn't. We hadn't even brought any rain gear with us. It wasn't coming down hard, but it was steady and wet. I told Ruth that we just as well get up and face the music - it wasn't going to get any better. It was still a little dark but we went and took our lines up and then were going to fix a little something to eat. Then we discovered the raccoons had taken our frying pan down the bank almost into the water and they had reached in our food box, which was a nice strong poultry box that was waxed and had holes in the ends used for handles. They had riddled a whole loaf of bread in the process of getting it out of the box. I guess we were lucky they didn't get the top off and ruin everything in there. Our stove was a little Optimus gas burner. The stove is 5 x 5 x 3 1/8 high and burns like a blowtorch. The skillet was a 6-inch diameter Teflon pan. We used these when we used to camp off motorcycles.

We had our jackets but we were wet through by now. We had one garbage bag that we cut holes in the corners and one in the middle. Ruth put this on for a rain top and served as a windbreaker. We went on through and when we got in the impoundment of the Upper Nueces Dam, we came to two fellows fishing. We stopped to talk and of course they could see that we were cold and wet. They told us that their camp was a half-mile down and they had left a fire burning and there was a coffee pot sitting beside it with coffee in it and for us to stop and help ourselves. We thanked them and went on. Before we got to their camp, we saw a drift pretty close to the water and I decided to set it on fire and warm up. I dug down in it until I found dry trash and got it going. Boy, that sure did feel good. We got warmed up and dried out pretty good. The rain had almost quit by now, so when we got to their camp we didn't stop. We headed on down lake and hoped whoever was going to pick us up would be there waiting. I really don't remember if we had to wait or not.

MOVING JUG

My grandson, Matthew, and I took the big boat and went to the river putting in at the Averhauff Landing. We went up stream several miles - almost as far as we could go - and we came up on a floating jug. It had some kind of fish on it. We just supposed someone was camped up that way and had set jug lines. We messed around fishing and catching minnows. Later, we decided to go back down river to spend the night. I guess we went at least halfway back and picked out a place to stop for the night. We had packed lunches and of course we slept in the boat. We baited our rod and reel lines and put them over the side. We hoped that we had picked a place that didn't have brush so we could do our lines like that. Sure enough, we caught three nice catfish that night. Seemed like about the time I'd get to sleep, a fish would bite. Anyway, it was fun. Next morning, here came that jug right on down the river. This time I told Matthew, "Let's see what's on that thing." Ok, we took it up and there was a medium sized gar on it. We dressed it out and put it with our collection. I think I've tried cooking only two needle nose gars and I find nothing wrong with them. Their flesh is very white and firm but seem to be very short of flavor. I've been told that the Alligator gar (wide bill) is the kind to eat. We fooled around that day and got a nice mess of pan fish to take home for supper.

TROUBLE THAT WASN'T TOO BAD HAD WE KNOWN

In the summer of 1997, Ed's boys, Chase and Bubba and I planned a boat trip to Amistad Lake north of Del Rio, Texas. We planned to stay three nights.

We launched the boat at the Box Canyon Ramp some ten miles up lake from Diablo East Ramp. The water between these two places is a very large body of water and gets very rough when the wind blows so by putting in at Box Canyon we get out of a lot of rough stuff. Now, I'm not saying it can't get bad farther up because it can.

This was July and it is plenty hot out there. There are no trees to get under. Depending on the time of day, sometimes you can get in the shade of a cliff or sometimes you can find a cave to get in. It's not like going on the Nueces River and having all those big oak trees and huge pecan trees shading you all day.

We went up lake to marker 23. Here the terrain levels out and you can choose the depth of water you want to fish in. It seems that the fish like shallow water to feed in but want deep water to escape into in case of danger (us). Chase got himself a real nice bass in this area, one to be proud of. There is a deep gulch off this marker that goes back in the Texas side and we go up in there and set a nice long trotline. Most always get several nice catfish in this place. When the lake is full, all this area is covered and you can find it only with a depth finder. Well, the first morning we took five nice cats off of our line. The law tells us on this lake that you can't fillet your fish in the field so that means you need more space or larger ice chests and more ice to store your fish. So, we decided to try keeping the fish alive by staking them out. When you do this, you take a chance on some one getting your fish. We put them on a bright red stringer and tied it to a nice strong limb sticking up out of the water. I put a note on the limb that said, "Please don't take our fish, we worked like everything to get them and we are coming back to get them. Thanks."

We had fished early in the morning and then ran our trotline and then ate breakfast. We fished some more until one or two in the afternoon. By now it is very hot so we go looking for some protection and I know a place. We go up to marker 25 and there is a gulch leading back into the Texas side. We go up three-quarters of a mile and drive right into a cave or an overhang. The water level has to be right to do this, mind you. Anyway, we take a nap and rest and then about 4:30 or so, we make a fish fry along with potatoes and whatever else. This is our big meal of the day. And then, we go back down to our fishing place and fish until dark. Now, we pick a place out of the wind if it's blowing and this is where we spend the night. We may set some of our gear out on the bank so the boat won't be quite so crowded. The two main seats let down into a lounge for Chase and me to sleep on and Bubba fixed his bed across the front seats. I really like camping like this - you stop for the night wherever you might be.

The next day went about the same - fish a while before breakfast and then go to our overhang and set out the heat of the day. We fixed another nice fish and potato fry and about 6 o'clock, go back fishing. We got back out in the main lake and the wind was pretty strong so we were unable to go fast - just about halfway planed off getting down within a half mile of our fishing area when the boat stopped. Just stopped going - the motor didn't stop - it was something with the drive line. I shifted it back and forth several times and got nothing. I had an outboard motor on back for trolling and emergencies like this but it had stopped on me this morning and I hadn't taken time to get it going again. I tried the outboard but nothing doing. We were drifting fast to Mexico right straight toward some rocks not more than two or three hundred yards away. There was a cove to our left but a little crosswind was working against us. I told the boys to grab a paddle and let's see if we could get into that cove. Boy, we worked at it and we made it into that cove. We missed the first little cove inside the big one but made it into the second. Bubba jumped out to tie the boat up and then he walked over a few yards and got up on a little knoll and hollered back, "Granddad, there is a boat coming!" I asked, "A Mexican boat or what?" He didn't know - just a boat. The boat pulled in the cove and they asked if we were in trouble. I said, "We sure are -

our drive is out." This fellow said that they were watching us and thought maybe we had trouble - said when they saw us paddling they were pretty sure we were in trouble. They towed us back to Texas - said they knew where we had spent the night before - did we want to go there? Sure, that'll be fine. After arriving there, we were visiting and he was telling us about some propeller trouble he had once and I told him about stripping out the splines in the drive hub on the motor where the out drive plugs into it just the year before. I told him I must not have gotten it lined up very well. He offered to tow us in to Box Canyon if we needed to go. He had already said that they were going in tomorrow morning. I told him no, we could wait until morning. We said something about having a trotline set up in the creek so he took us over there and we took it up. He said they were camped just around the next point and would come in the morning and tow us in.

I told the boys that I was going to get in the water and work on that outboard motor and get it working. They said they'd clean the fish while I did that. Ok, I took the carburetor off and cleaned a little trash out and it seemed to run all right.

The boys would take a fish off the stringer and just lay the rest of them in the water. Then they'd take another off and lay the rest down in the water. Then, when there was only one fish left on the stringer, they put it back in the water and it swam off and took the stringer with it. Right about then, I wouldn't have cared if they had lost all of them.

It was late by now - after 9 PM, and I was hoping the boys would forget about being hungry, but they didn't. "We're hungry." OK, we fixed some sandwiches.

I woke up in the middle of the night and was laying there thinking about the boat and how it acted after it seemingly quit. I remembered that it stayed pointing into the wind with the engine idling. Anytime your power is off, a boat will turn cross ways to the wind right quick. I thought it could be the rubber bushing in the propeller that might be stripped. I'll find out as soon as daylight comes. When day broke, I was in the water. I put the shift in forward and got back to the drive and proceeded to turn the prop. At first I thought, no it's not that, and then I put everything I had on it and I was able to turn it and the motor was not turning. Boy, what a relief - all I had to do to be back in business was to change the prop. After this happening to us makes me think that I should carry enough rope to be able to anchor in deep water. If you could anchor, you could get in the water and change a prop. I'd want a life jacket on and tie a cord on my tools and on the extra prop and maybe on me to keep the wind from blowing me away from the boat. I'd get it changed - you could bet on that.

We went ahead and ate breakfast in case those people came to tow us. After eating, we fired up the boat and it worked! We fired the little motor and it worked too. Well, we fished around in the area close by so if they came, they'd see us. After a while, we tootled around the next point where they were. They were packing up their stuff getting ready to go. I told them that we had ours fixed. We thanked them over and over for helping us in time of trouble. They asked us if we were going to stay another night. I said that we had planned to stay another night but I thought we were going to run out of ice. He said they had lots of ice that they didn't need and gave us a big chunk of it. He even gave us a couple catfish. I got their address and name. Later, I wrote them a Thank You note and Ed finally got the boys to write them too. I tell you what, I just couldn't thank them enough.

We left them and stayed pretty close to shore trolling going in and out of most of the coves. After while Bubba caught a real nice shell cracker. That's just a big ole perch and fights hard for a little while. After we got that thing put up, we hadn't gone fifty yards and he hollered, "Granddad, I really got something on now, he's really pulling hard!" I stopped the boat and even backed up a little so he could gain on the fish. The thing was pulling down deep so I knew it wasn't a large mouth bass. When he got it close to the boat, it went under the boat and I was afraid the line would get caught on the drive. Somehow, Chase took the rod from him and got him over on his side. Then Bubba came over and took it again. He got it up and we netted it and what do you think it was? It was a 21-inch stripper - a really nice fish. That made Bubba pretty happy.

It was a little after noon now and was getting plenty hot. I pulled in the bay off marker 22 and went to a place where there wasn't so much wind. The boys got the minnow seine out and started playing with it. I think they had about as much fun with it as they did fishing. Bubba said he didn't know they made such things. I had put the top up and was trying to catch a little shuteye, but the kids had to check on me once in a while - to see if I was sleeping. In a little while Chase came over and said, "Granddad, there is a houseboat out in the lake - see if you can get him on the radio." I turn the radio on and called, "House boat." He answered right away. He asked me where I was. I told him that I was back in the bay off marker 22. He asked what kind of boat we were in. I told him. First though, he thought I was the Coast Guard. Evidently he had been calling the Coast Guard and when I called him, he thought they were answering him. When he found out that I was not the Coast Guard, he asked what kind of boat we were in. He said we could travel faster than he - would I go down lake calling the Guard and when I was able to reach them, tell them there had been a drowning up at marker 25. I told him, sure, I'd do that. So, we headed down lake calling and calling for the Guard and in a little while, Box Canyon answered me. I explained what the score was and he suggested that he try calling the Guard. He was up on top of the hill and he called them and got them. I could read him as he talked but couldn't hear the Guard. He called me back and told me the Coast Guard would be up as soon as they could. I guess it was about an hour, I heard the Guard call Box Canyon. After they signed off, I called the Guard and told them that I was the one who had relayed the message from the houseboat. They wanted to know what the houseboat's number was. I told them that I had not gotten that information. We signed off and I didn't hear anything more about it.

We tootled up Cow Creek and picked a place out of the wind and spent the night. That evening however, we heard thunder - couldn't tell much about it as the sky was overcast. Next morning, we had more thunder and closer too. I told the boys, let's eat breakfast and head home. That suited them so that's what we did. We arrived home at 12 noon.

TOO MANY FISH

Ruth and I took our 14-foot flat bottom jon boat loaded with our gear and launched at Averhauff Landing and went up river past the backwater and on beyond a couple rapids. The river was running strong enough that we could motor up the rapids. We set up camp alongside a long rapid that spilled into a real nice hole. Upstream there is a nice piece of water that I've heard called "Blue Hole" and I suppose it's a half to three-quarters of a mile long. We set a couple trotlines up above and one in the hole below. Next morning, we checked our lines upstream, which produced nothing, but the one below paid off. We had several nice catfish on this line. I tied up on the deep side where the swift water was coming off the rapids and I told Ruth to drop her line in to see if she could catch a fish while I cleaned fish. OK, she started catching fish and I hardly had time to clean on the fish - she was getting them faster than I could clean 'em. I finally told her to put her pole up so I could catch up.

We had seen Billy Franks fly over a couple times. He was crop spraying in a farm a little north and east of us. I was talking to him later and was telling him about us fishing up there. He told me that he had seen someone's camp up there that sure did show up from the air. They had a striped tent - blue and yellow striped - sure was pretty. I told him that was ours - I had put up a 10 x 20 foot shade and our tent was under it.

I started telling everyone that I'd never take my wife fishing again because she made so much noise in the boat and besides, she caught more fish than I did. Ha ha, really true, too.

FINDING THE FISH'S HIDING PLACES

We don't fish for crappie much anymore - it seems like you can't get them like we used too. Of course there are lots more people fishing these days.

There was a friend visiting me and he wanted to go fishing up on the river. We went up in my big boat and I thought of a strategy that I wanted to try. Leon thought I was crazy but I told him to just wait a little bit before he started condemning me. What I did was to go along watching my depth finder and finding some underwater brush that couldn't be seen from above. I found what seemed to be some pretty good brush. I tied a rope across the river and then we could tie the boat on each end to that rope out over the brush. Leon said, "There is no brush here." I told him, "Oh yes there is." Anyway, we started fishing and he got hung up right away. I asked him what was wrong. Well he said, "There is brush down there." I told him he would have to let his line straight down and not drag it like he was used to doing at home. Here you're not fishing for crappie unless you're in a treetop. We got a few crappie here and then we went and found another underwater brush pile and got a few more.

I've heard said, one reason why the crappie are fading out is because they lay their eggs on logs in the water and all the speed boats, ski boats and jet ski machines cause so much action in the water that it keeps the eggs knocked off the logs. Who knows?

WHEN TROLLING, HANG ON TO YOUR ROD

One time Bruce Ivey and I were over on Amistad Lake. We were back in the Cow Creek area camped and fishing. The lake was full, and when it is, there is an awful lot of shoreline. When trolling I try to stay fairly close to the bank. Of course in case of shallow water you have to get farther out in order not to drag bottom. In other words, you have to play it by ear. When the wind is blowing – and it is most of the time - you have to keep your hands on the steering wheel every second. The wind will take you into the rock very quickly. Well, ole Bruce had laid his rod down on the gunwale to rest or do something, and about that time a fish hit it or it caught on a snag and jerked right off the boat. I guess he saw it move or started off and he hollered at me to stop. I couldn't have stopped or we would have been in the rocks in no time flat.

Some years later when the water had gone down several feet, I walked that shoreline to see if I might find his rod. The area was very brushy and I didn't find it.

Gary Kinnard used to like to beach comb after the water had gone down several feet hunting stuff. He has found as many as six rods and reels in one stay over there. He had picked up a number of anchors too. A lot of people do just like Bruce did, get tired and lay it down and away it goes if a fish strikes or it catches on brush.

Once Ruth and I were across from Diablo East over in Castle Canyon and I was walking the shoreline casting, and I found a real nice closed face Diawa reel and a rod on it. I'd sit on a rock and cast an area and then move to another sitting place and cast that area. One place there I noticed a little round thing sticking up out of the sand a little with the water lapping over it and I thought it looked like a reel handle. Sure enough it was. This one cleaned up real good - wasn't a thing wrong with it.

TROUBLE WITH BOTH TRAILERS

About four years ago I sold all my cattle. I engaged Rodney Chitty to haul one load of cattle for me. He had a nice 24-foot gooseneck trailer and, I suppose, around seven feet wide. My trailer was 18 x 6 1/2. I had it figured if he hauled one load and I haul one load that afternoon then I'd haul the rest of them the next morning. I backed up to the chute first so Rodney would have to help me load. He said, "You know I'd help you load any way." We ran too many cattle up the chute and couldn't close the middle gate. Rodney said, "It don't matter, you're going to put in a full load anyway." I really knew better than to do that but I let it go. We filled the trailer up and I moved it away so Rodney could back his trailer up to the chute. We loaded him up and he took off heading to Uvalde. I think I had to air some tires up before leaving.

My trailer was a little high in front when loaded and that wasn't good. My trailer used to sag a little low in front so Ed warped it to where the hitch went down lower and then when raised up to the hitch on the truck, the front of the trailer is a little too high. Well, it didn't take long for the cattle to shift to the rear and that meant the back of the trailer was much heavier than the front and was lifting up on the truck. Of course that meant that all the weight of the trailer, cattle and part of the truck weight was on the trailer. Tom Fatherree was with me and I told him that I wasn't going to go over 20 miles an hour. Going any faster than that would be very dangerous with the thing out of balance that much. Well, we didn't get more than two miles and a tire went out on the trailer. The right rear on the trailer blew and that really lifted the back of the truck. I pulled off the highway - well, I didn't get completely off until I put the truck in four wheel drive and low range and dragged it off. The right rear of the trailer was digging into the ground. I was wondering what in the world we were going to do. I looked up ahead and saw a road coming off the highway and it was built up so I thought, oh boy, I'll pull up on that and when the truck goes down on the other side with the trailer still up on the road, that thing will level off. Sure enough, it worked real good. We were able to push the cattle to the front of the trailer and then I tied a chain across behind them to keep them from working back again to the rear when we got on the road again. Now it was time to put the spare on. The old spare wasn't much but was all I had.

Tom and I were working on changing the wheel when Rodney showed up. I said, "Man, you sure made a quick trip to Uvalde and back." He said he never got there yet - said his rig is up ahead about a mile, in fact you can see it from here.

What happened was; he was going along and right after he met this car (of course the car had nothing to do with what happened but did get involved) a wheel came off the left rear of his trailer. He pulled off in the ditch and about that time, the driver of this car, mad as the dickens, came up and wanted to know why he threw this bolt through his windshield. Well, the wheel on Rodney's trailer had gotten loose and was breaking the lug bolts off and one of them went through this guy's windshield. Rodney told him he sure was sorry and that it sure wasn't intentional. Anyway the fellow calmed down and was giving Rodney a ride to town when they saw us in trouble and stopped to see what our problem was. They went on then and Tom and I got our wheel on and headed out again. My rig was much better balanced now but I still took it easy because I was scared of my old spare.

We made it to the stockyard at Uvalde and got unloaded and on the way out of Uvalde there was a tire shop that I stopped at and bought a tire. This guy sold me the tire, mounted it and put it on the ground all for ten bucks. I couldn't believe my ears. It was a well worn tire but I had only one more load of cattle to take to market then I would be through with the trailer. The old tire held up and I see it's still on the trailer - I hauled one heifer from the Vet's for Ed the other day. I want to tell you one thing for sure, though, I closed that middle gate on that last load.

On the way back from Uvalde, Rodney's trailer was still there in the ditch. I sure hated to see the cattle crowded up in there in the hot sun, but what else could I do? He had to get a hub as well as a wheel for his rig. He got the cattle to the stock pens late that afternoon.

OH, SO GENTLE CATTLE

I bought a bunch of calves from Henry and Mary Ann Daly one year. I also bought three head from John Carpenter. John had a hand fed Holstein that I paid one price for and he had two other calves out of the same cow. One was about two years old weighing about 800 pounds and the younger one was what I called an oat calf. The mama cow was a red whiteface and half Brahman. When we were trying to pen them, the larger calf headed for parts unknown. We went ahead and loaded and went in and weighed them. The ones I bought from John had to be weighed separately as I was paying him different prices. Henry's cattle were at John's place, too.

We went to the railroad pens that were north of Crystal about a mile. We had to unload and run the cattle around a lane and then into the scales. The weighing went OK. Mary Ann said I didn't need to put her calves in my pens to wean them as they were all very gentle and tame and they all had names. OK, so we turned them out in the field. I did brand them, however. The next morning we went to church and when I got home, Earl Taylor, who had a place across the river from me, called me and asked if I had some new calves. I said, "Yes I did - just put them in on my oats yesterday." He said, "There is a bunch of them in my place." Well, those cattle crossed two fences and the river and another fence into his place. You remember they didn't need weaning. The next day or so, John Carpenter called me and said he had that one animal in the pen and I could come and get her. I said OK, but I wanted to brand her after I got her in my trailer just in case she jumped out of the trailer or something. Henry was with me and we went to the railroad pens to weigh her so I could pay John. It was getting close to dark when we got there. We unloaded her and ran her around the lane to the scales. We weighed her and turned her out in a pen so we could take her back to the trailer. She was really upset and I told Henry and John not to get in the pen with her. The first thing she did was to climb up the steps that goes along the chute that goes to the train cars. I hollered at John and told him that's why I wanted to brand her at his place. I really thought she would jump to the ground outside the pens but she jumped back into the pen. I went around the pen climbing over fences to open a gate so we could get her back to the trailer. You know what, Henry got in the pen with her to come across to keep from climbing over a couple fences and all at once I heard a noise. It was Henry running with that animal right behind him. He jumped up on the fence just in time and the calf crashed into the fence just under him. I told him I didn't think he was that crazy. He told me that it was dark and he didn't think the calf could see him.

Every time I got these cattle up to do any work on them, this one whiteface, part Brahman animal would break away from the herd. I found out there was no use to try running after her, because doing that, some of the others would break. Just let her go and she would come back and get in the herd and that was a lot better than roping her and then having a big job on your hands. I don't think I ever had all gentle cattle. Seems there always had to be some wild ones to keep you on your toes.

DELIVERING CATTLE AT MIDNIGHT

A number of years ago our Pastor, Ross Davis, wanted to help me work cattle and haul some to the Cotulla auction. We got the cattle up in late afternoon when it wasn't quite so hot. We got them penned and then ran them through the chute. We were vaccinating all of them and we were cutting and branding the bull calves and branding the heifers. The ones I wanted to sell were cut out and put in the holding pen. By the time we got through, it was late. We loaded a trailer full and came in town and ate supper. It must have been near 11 PM by the time we headed out to Cotulla. After we unloaded at the auction pens I said something about being tired. Ross asked me if I wanted him to drive home. I told him sure, if he wanted to. The auction there is about three miles south of Cotulla on I-35. We came back up I-35 and then got on the Big Wells road. I guess nearly a mile out we saw some deer run across the road and then when we got to where they had been, here comes two more and both of them slammed into the side of the truck. One was a buck and he hit the truck over the right front wheel and the other, a doe, hit right about the front of the door on the right side. We turned around and went back. The doe lay dead, but no buck. We picked the doe up and brought it home. If nothing else, she would sure make some good dog meat.

On the way home, Ross said, "It sure would be something in the morning to read in the San Antonio News that the Pastor of First Baptist and the Chairman of his deacons were picked up for being in possession of a doe deer at night and out of season." I told Ross not to even think of anything like that. Surely, we could have talked our way out of it. Never can tell, though, it might depend on what kind of mood the warden was in. He could throw the book at you too. Ole deer hitting something like that sure gets bruised bad. Of course the dogs don't mind.

Next morning Bruce Ivey went with me to take another load to the auction. On the way back, we stopped where the deer had clobbered the truck and I found my hub cap that the buck had knocked off. He knocked the clearance light out too on that right front.

LOSING CATTLE FROM NEGLECT

I stock farmed because it was the easiest thing I could do and do the custom farming that I did. Cattle seemed to take care of themselves pretty well. I lost a cow now and then and I would loose a heifer in calving from time to time. I just thought that could be expected.

One year, I had a nice bunch of heifers that were going to calve for the first time. My fields were green and nice and the cattle were very fat. I was very busy doing custom farming and just didn't look after them as I should have. I lost ten of them that year. That really hurt but was my fault.

Sometime after that and I can't remember just when, I found a nice yearling dead just a few feet from where it had watered. I went by Dr. Darter's and told him about it. He said he thought he better go out and look at it. The yearling looked to have bogged in the mud part way up to its knees, watered and backed out and died right there and showed no signs of struggle. Dr. Darter took his scalpel and made an incision under the front leg on the side of the chest where the skin is tender. He pealed the skin back a little and said, "Yeah, there it is. That's a clostridium." He named which one but I don't remember which one. He asked me if I had been vaccinating these cattle. I told him that I had not because I raised these cattle and had not been importing any cattle in at all. He asked me about buzzards and coyotes and even other birds. Well, I knew exactly what he was saying - I just hadn't been thinking of it. Clostridium have a spore and any animal or bird can transport it very easily. He told me to get these cattle vaccinated *today* and he meant **today.** He also told me to get that animal burned and burned good.

I will always appreciate him coming out to take a look. He most likely saved me an awful lot of grief.

A BULLET THAT HIT ITS MARK

Out at our farm several years ago I was welding in a pipeline from my river pump up to the discharge where it emptied into a concrete ditch. I had the right-of-way cleaned off and smoothed and I had a pit dozed out so I could pull the pipes over it to weld them together. For a while, I could turn the pipes, thereby be able to do the welding from the top. After the pipe got long and down over the hill it couldn't be turned anymore so I would have to go around and under it to weld. That is why I had the pit dozed out so I could get under it to weld.

One day one of Eddie's friends came over to see what we were doing. It was Tim Darter, who's dad owned the pasture to the west and north of us. Tim had been up in Austin, Texas, visiting some of his kin and had bought himself a handgun. It was a military revolver that used the regular .45 army ammo. I told Tim to let me see that gun and I'd see if it was any good. He handed it to me and I loaded it and I said, "See that clod of dirt down there?" I guess the clod was 'bout 60 feet away. I took aim, fired and busted that clod. I handed the gun back to Tim and told him that I guessed the gun was pretty good.

Later on that evening after he had gone, Eddie told me that Tim said to him, "Man, your Daddy didn't hit to the left or right or over or under that clod, he hit it straight on. Man alive, he can shoot!" Well, just between you and me, I'm sure glad he didn't ask me to do it again.

A VERY SURPRISED ROPER

I was doing some custom farming for a rancher by the name of A. M. Harkey. Mr. Harkey lived in Mason, Texas, and ranched near there. He also had holdings here in Zavala County that lay east and a little south of Crystal City. One place was the old Sam Ward farm. Another place he had was south of there along the Brundage highway. One day I went out to check on a job we were doing on the Ward place and Mr. Harkey was there. He told me there was an old cow in one of the fields that he wanted to get out and for me to get in the back of his pickup and he would put me on the cow and for me to rope her. I told him that I was no roper and that he might throw me out of the pickup. He told me to get in there and when he got up on the cow for me to put that rope on her. OK, away we went - the field the cow was in had a waterhole with thick brush around it and that is where the cow hung out except to feed. When we drove down there we could see the cow about two hundred yards out away from the waterhole, so here we go after her. Of course when the cow realized we were coming at her she headed for the water hole and brush. Well, we just barely got up on her as she was about to enter the brush and Mr. Harkey hollering, "Put that rope on her!" I had a loop built and was swinging and threw at the cow and to my surprise, more than the cow's, I caught her. It surprised me so much, I don't really remember just how I held her. I might have tied the rope to the headache rack on the truck but thinking about it, that might have jerked the thing off the truck, so I must have jumped out of the truck and went around a tree with the rope. I don't really remember. At any rate, we went after the trailer and loaded her up.

QUESTION ABOUT HOW TO LOAD A BRAHMAN BULL

I bought a Brahman bull from Travis Box to put with my herd. This bull was twenty months old and ready for service. The bull was gentle and would come to me anywhere in the fields if I had a bucket of feed. One time my grandson, Matthew, and I were walking down a road along side of a field and he was carrying a bucket with range cubes in it. We were walking along talking and he wasn't paying any attention to anything other than what we were talking about. The bull came up on us from behind and put his big head down over Matthew's shoulder to get some feed. When he saw that big head, he jumped sideways and started to run. When he realized what was happening, he stopped and let Mr. Bull have some feed.

One time my bull had gotten across the fence into Darter's pasture and was fighting with a much smaller white faced bull. In the fight, my bull got pushed into the fence, which was a net wire construction, and fell. He just laid there so I took a chain and put it around his horns and pulled him with my pickup back on my side. Well, he just laid there for a while and after a while, I thought, maybe he is dead. At first I figured he was playing possum as I had seen Brahman cattle do. A bunch of my cattle had gathered up pretty close to see what was going on when after several minutes, the bull jumped up and went into the herd of cattle nearby.

I'd had the bull for about twelve years and thought it was time to sell him. I didn't know just how I was going to load him as I had had him in the crowding pen several times in the past and there was no way he was going to go through the chute. If I had to give him a shot of some kind, I would pop it to him real quick with an automatic device through the fence. Knowing I had to get him through the chute in order to get him in my trailer, I had to figure out a way to do it.

I built a gate full length of the crowding pen hinging it at the edge of the chute on the angle side of the pen. On the other end I mounted a sheave so I could double line to get a double pull on the gate. OK, I got the bull in the pen headed the right direction and alone. I pulled the gate over against him which placed him already in the chute and in line straight to the trailer. OK, Mr. Bull, you're going now. I figured I'd have all kinds of trouble getting him to go, but I didn't. I popped him one time and on into the trailer he went. No Problem. I closed him in the front part of the trailer and he stood there for the whole time we worked some more cattle and got more cut out to go to market with him. There wasn't any kind of problem until we drove in close to the auction in Uvalde. When he heard all those cattle bawling he came unglued. I thought he was going to tear up my trailer or jump out. When we got into the unloading place, he couldn't get out of that trailer fast enough. I'm glad I wasn't the one running him down the lane. That was the last I saw of him. He weighed something over nineteen hundred pounds. I got my check for the cattle a couple days later.

You know, I felt kinda bad after the way he acted. You'd a thought he was a two-year-old but I knew better.

FAST FLYING AIRPLANE IS GOING TO BE LATE

Today is July 12, 1999. My grandson, Chase, and I are on our way home from San Antonio. We just left I-35 getting on highway 57 which will take us to La Pryor and then go left on highway 83 bringing us home to Crystal City.

We took my daughter, Nancy, to the airplane - her flight was scheduled for 1:30 PM. We left home around 9 AM heading to San Antonio. I had to return an oxygen bottle to a supplier at Wurzbach and Fredericksburg Road. That put us in the vicinity of a Luby's cafeteria, so we decided to have lunch there.

After lunch, we took Nancy to the Airport getting her there an hour early. It takes about an hour to get your ticket checked, your luggage checked in and find the gate you're supposed to enter to get to the plane.

After all that was done, Chase and I headed southwest. We stopped out south of San Antonio at a big service station located at I-35 and 1604 to fuel up.

The night Nancy came, she was supposed to arrive in San Antonio at 10 PM. Ed was going up to get her and he went early because he was going to visit a friend. At the time she was supposed to depart Nashville she found out the plane was going to be an hour late. She was informed the plane hadn't left Chicago yet. I called Ed on his mobile phone and told him. He was in the south edge of San Antonio when I got him and he said he'd call the airport and find out what the arrival time was. I left it with him. I don't know just what time she arrived - all I know is it put them in here after 3 AM. She slept a little late that morning I should say. She got in to visit with us about 10 AM that morning.

As Chase and I were coming home he asked me where did I think we would be if we didn't have automobiles. I told him that we sure wouldn't be going to San Antonio two days in a row. Nancy and I had taken Ruth to the doctor the day before is why I say - two days in a row. I told Chase that we'd be on foot, horse back, burro or team and wagon. I guess making a trip riding in a wagon, it would take at least six days plus the time doing what you had to do when you got there. I don't reckon many of us would like to go back to them good old days.

I told Chase about the first time I went to San Antonio. It was back about 1932. The pastor of our church had a nice bunch of boys in his Royal Ambassador Chapter and he treated them by taking them to San Antonio. At that time my Dad had his own school bus (I spoke of it before) and the preacher got him to haul the boys up there, so I got to go. I was too young but I had to go with Mom and Dad. We went to the Brackenridge Park to have our lunch and then in the afternoon, we went to the Majestic Theater and saw a movie. The name of the movie was "Frank Buck, Bring 'em Back Alive." That was my first movie ever. That theater was something too. You looked up and it was just like looking up into the sky. All the stars and everything were up there. After the movie, he took us to the Buck Horn Saloon. That was really something. It was like a museum - the thing that stuck in my mind was the big buck deer with a giant rack of antlers. Seems like in later years they moved this museum into the Lone Star Brewery lobby. I believe that big deer is still around.

On the way home, we stopped out east of Uvalde at a place called Honey Hut and feasted on ice cream. The Honey Hut used to be three miles out of Uvalde but now, the town has spread a good ways out beyond the Hut. You know, I don't know if my Mom and Dad had ever been to San Antonio before that or not. I don't remember them ever talking about it.

EVEN I WOULDN'T HAVE
BELIEVED THIS ONE HAD I NOT LOOKED

On the opening day of deer season in 1997, Tom Fatherree and I went out to the farm to watch for deer. Tom took the south stand on "the hump" and I went to the tall stand on the west.

A little after daylight I saw 3 deer coming from the river going west. They were about 400 yards north of me - in the north side of the Coastal Bermuda grass field. Finally I saw antlers on the one in the lead so I decided to take a crack at him. I did and missed. They ran back east toward the river with this one I'd shot at in the rear. I could see his antlers real good now as he ran and felt worse and worse that I had missed him. When they got over next to the road that goes to the house they stopped. However, I couldn't see the other two, only the one I had shot at. Evidently he was standing on one of those big borders that ran north and south facing south just a short distance from the concrete ditch that goes west and east. There were some big bunches of Blue Panicum grass along the ditch there, but he had stopped just right. He was lined up just to the south of a big pecan tree that I had cut down in the northeast corner of the field that I was in. I looked and looked at that deer for 10 minutes it seemed like. For a long time I was not considering taking a crack at him but after he just kept standing there, I decided that I just as well take a shot - maybe he would run back toward me. I raised up over him about a body's thickness over his shoulders and touched it off. He ran and jumped the cement ditch and fence on it's edge and disappeared in the Johnson grass to the south. Then I saw the other two jump both fences along the road and disappear. I didn't even entertain the idea that I hit the deer or even come close to hitting him. The distance was five to six hundred yards.

A little earlier, I had heard Tom shoot down below. After my episode I looked down his way and I saw him standing at the edge of my field. I stepped out of my stand and waved to him to come on. He came and told me that he had gotten a nice little buck west of him - a place we had been putting out corn. I told him what I had done - scared 'em off. We got in the truck and went up and around the Bermuda grass over to the road going up to the house and down that way. I wouldn't have gone that way but Terry was down in the turkey stand and we had to go get her. I was telling Tom about the deer I shot at and showed him as we lined up with my stand over there and the old pecan tree that had been cut down and the space between the clumps of Panicum grass. He said, "Sure, that was a long one." Well, as I started up, I thought to myself, wouldn't that be something if that deer was laying there just the other side of that fence. Well, believe it or not, he was laying there. He had jumped the fence and turned toward the river and there he was to my surprise.

When we got down to Terry's stand she told us that after I shot last, there were two deer come running past her doing at least 105 miles per hour and they were both bucks.

We went down and got Tom's deer and took them to where we field dress 'em and then on home where we skinned them and cut them down the back and hung 'em up. We congratulated each other on this opening day hunt. I wish Terry had nailed one of those that she saw.

SOMETIMES YOU JUST CAN'T CONNECT

Later in the season of '97, Chase, Bubba and I were out at the farm hunting. Chase took the stand on the hump on the south and Bubba and I got in the tall stand on the west. After while, we heard Chase shoot. In a little bit he shot again. And then some more. In a little bit we saw him walking east inside the edge of the field and ever once in a while, he'd shoot again. We wondered what in the world was he shooting at. He must have shot 10 - 12 times. I decided maybe we better go see. Well, Bubba was out of our stand and took off down there on foot. I got in the truck and went down and drove across the field to where Chase finally came to a stop.

He had a spike buck about midway up the field. Chase said the deer came out away up at the corner about where the gate is at the end of the county road. Said the deer was coming down the road for a while and then came over into the field still coming toward him and then he got out of the stand and walked toward the deer shooting at him ever little bit. Chase finally won, though. We didn't have to grind this deer. Chase had already made hamburger out of him.

On another occasion Chase shot a real nice 8 pointer out of that hump stand. It was all the way across the patch of brush to the south in the edge of the next field. That was property belonging to the Nueces Pecan Farm. Ed was the foreman there, so there was no problem getting the deer. We drove out to the highway; went a mile south and back east to that field and up to his deer. That's the way I like to do it.

WHAT YOU CALL " DEAD IN THE WATER"

About five years ago (I know saying five years ago doesn't mean anything unless you know that I am writing this February 29, 2000) Jim Cottle and I went over to Amistad Lake near Del Rio, Texas, to fish and camp. We took my boat and pickup. We packed everything we needed including food and water and we fueled up the boat and truck and headed out.

We launched the boat at Diablo East Boat Ramp and parked the truck and trailer up in the parking lot. Diablo East is on the Devil's River so we motor down to the Rio Grande and turned up lake there. We were cruising along at a pretty good clip when Jim hollered, "Hey, our cups blew out!" I slowed and turned around to go get our cups and then I stopped when we got to them. Jim picked them up and I gave the boat the gas but all that happened was the motor speeded up and the boat "no go." We didn't have a lot of time because we were drifting toward Mexico which wasn't over a quarter of a mile away and there were jagged rocks over there. Luckily I had the 9 ½ horse power outboard on and I fired it up and headed to the Texas side. I hadn't taken time to put it down or to trip its pad and lower it so the prop would be just below the bottom of the boat so it could bite the water and go. Like it was, it was cavitating real bad but we made it into a cove on the Texas side. The best I could tell by feeling back behind the big motor, the shaft wasn't turning that drives the out drive. Due to power failure, we camped right there.

We walked the shore fishing and had pretty good luck. We caught more than we could eat for supper.

The next morning Jim asked me if we were going to fish any before we started back. I told him sure, we could fish awhile. We were walking the shore again and doing pretty good. All this time I kept thinking that we should be puttering down lake using the outboard while the wind wasn't so bad. It was pretty quiet until about 10 AM and then the wind was coming up. I thought , boy, we blew it. Well, you know, by noon the wind had calmed and we had a perfect situation for going in with the outboard. I guess we were 15 or more miles up lake and several past Box

Canyon Ramps. At first I was thinking about going in to Box Canyon and catching a ride with someone going toward Del Rio and dropping me off there at Diablo East which is not far off the highway. We started out and things were going very smoothly and when we got even with Box Canyon the water was very calm and things going very well so we decided to "go for it." I was going from marker to marker or cutting across when I could. We even were trolling as we went and we caught several stripers out there in that deep water.

We had one six gallon tank of outboard gas and I told Jim that wouldn't be near enough to get to Diablo East. I had an electric fuel pump on the big engine gasline so we rigged it up so we could pump gas into a two-gallon paint bucket. I also had a quart of outboard oil so Jim pumped gas and mixed it in the bucket and with the help of a funnel put it in the outboard tank. We had it down pat. After we turned up the Devil's River we stopped and fished awhile. I caught one nice bass and Jim found a good rod and reel. After fishing here a while, we went on up the Devil's River and decided to go across from Diablo East into Castle Canyon and fish and we even spent the night there. Just before dark, we ran into the dad burndest bunch of some kind of gnats. We couldn't get away from them because the outboard wouldn't push the boat fast enough to get away from them. They quit bothering us after dark. We didn't dare turn a light on for fear they'd come to it.

The next morning we were fishing from the boat and one cove we went into, Jim got two nice stripers right quick and then they were gone. Those stripers are about like the whites, they run the bait fish up to the top of the water and they'll hit almost anything you throw at them.

We loaded up a little before noon and came home. In a few days, I backed the boat in under the truck port and pulled the motor. Sure enough, the hub that is mounted on the flywheel was stripped out. I went to San Antonio to get one and they informed me that it was an old model and they would have to find one. They finally found one out in California somewhere to the tune of $350.00 bucks. Yeah, that little hub with four bolt holes about 5 inches in diameter. Playthings do cost!

AN AFTERNOON/EVENING DEER HUNT

On December 18, 2000, my grandson, Chase (our son Ed's older boy) came by to get me and take me hunting out to one of his friend's place. First we moved a couple large hay bales down along the edge of the oat field to use as a blind. After moving the bales we went back in the truck and parked it up the field a pretty good ways and walked back to the hay bales. We sat there until almost dark without seeing anything. We were walking back to the truck when we saw two deer up the other side of the truck. Chase stopped right there and I moved over to my right and got the truck in between me and the deer. I got to the truck and the deer were still there looking in our direction. I couldn't get a very good rest in the position I was in and besides, the deer were right in line with some houses on the other side. It ended up that I didn't shoot at all and the deer vanished in the near dark. Of course Chase wondered why I didn't shoot knowing that I had gotten to the truck and should have had a good chance. I explained to him that I didn't have a real good chance and about the houses on the other side.

The next afternoon about 4:30 we went back out there and he sat behind the bales and I went up to where we had seen the deer the evening before and found a place to back the truck into the edge of the brush and sat in the truck thinking those deer might come out again about where they had the day before. About 5:15 I heard Chase shoot and then he shot again 'long about 6:00 and then in a few minutes, he let 'er rip again. By now, it was good dark so I fired up and drove down to where he was. He had walked to his first deer but didn't touch it because he wanted to tag it before he did anything. He told me that he had gone to the first one and was fixing to tag it when he heard a noise to the south of him and when he turned and looked he saw a nice buck and could skylight his antlers against the western sky. He said he (Chase) made a sort of a funny noise in his throat and the deer came straight toward him. The deer stopped facing toward him and he touched one off and the deer went down. He hadn't gone to this deer yet when I arrived. After I arrived, he filled out his two tags and we walked out and tagged to first one and then walked over to the other. When we got close, the deer flopped. I reached down to grab his antler so I could cut his throat but he jerked it out of my hand. This happened two or three times and then the deer got his front feet under himself and for an instant, I thought he was trying to charge us. Then, he got all four of his feet under himself and was up and gone to parts unknown. The weeds were up to knee high and our little three-cell flashlight was very weak so we went back to the first buck and Chase dragged him to the truck. On the way I told Chase to let this be a lesson, never go to a downed deer without your rifle. He asked me what I would have done if I had had my rifle. I told him I would have shot him again. We got in the truck and drove around and around in the weeds to see if we could jump the deer, but to no avail. Going back to the first one, we dressed him out and loaded him in the truck. I then turned the truck around and headed out to go home but the truck seemed funny and I told Chase something was wrong with the truck. I stopped and took a look at the tires and sure enough the left front tire was as flat as a flitter. Well, Chase got under the back of the truck and got the spare out and we proceeded to change the flat. With all this done, we headed home and believe it or not, we made it this time.

You know, the split second of highly concentrated fun in pulling that trigger sure causes a hunter an awful lot of work. Did you ever think of it that way?

ABOUT THE AUTHOR

Dale Walker was born in 1924 in Crystal City, Zavala County, Texas. In the spring of 1930 his family moved on a farm on the Nueces River seven miles north of Crystal City. Dale was taught farming operations using teams of horses to plant and cultivate with. The heavier work was done with a 10-20 McCormick Deering tractor. Later, a small International (culti-vision) tractor was purchased and this little tractor was worth two or three teams of horses.

Dale graduated from Hi-School in 1943 and early in 1944 he went to serve his country. He served in the European Theater of Operations with the Air Communication System as a high speed radio operator. He communicated with outgoing and incoming aircraft to their midpoint and from their midpoint of their destination using International Morse Code.

Dale married Ruth Powell January 1, 1946. After returning from the service late in 1946 they both returned to Crystal City where Ruth went to work as a Laboratory and X-ray Technician and Dale went into the service station business. He sold the station after a year and went back into the business he knew best. He started doing hay-baling, plowing and all sorts of custom farming. In 1970 they bought the home place where they stock farmed to take up Dale's spare time. During all this, they raised three beautiful children. Ruth and Dale both retired in the 90's and are now living "happily ever after" enjoying their children and grandchildren and great grandchildren.

ADDITIONAL COPIES OF
RAMBLIN' ON

TO PURCHASE ADDITIONAL COPIES SEND $21.95 PLUS
$2.00 FOR POSTAGE AND HANDLING - MONEY ORDER
OR CHECK. PLEASE ALLOW AMPLE TIME FOR CHECKS
TO CLEAR.
SEND TO:

MATTHEW STEWART
4161 Hi-way 35 North
ROCKPORT, TEXAS 78382

Telephone 361 729 9863
E-mail   mstewart@pyramid3.net